The
Christmas
Redemption:
A Courtroom Adventure

For Gordon,

My writing
buddy. Keep it
up.

Julia

Address your requests to landiswrites@gmail.com or to the publisher at the address given below.

Cover and interior illustrations by
Susanne Discenza Frueh, sfrueh@gmail.com

Book Design by Frogtown Bookmaker
frogtownbookmaker.com

Published by Lystra Books & Literary Services, LLC
391 Lystra Estates Drive, Chapel Hill, NC 27517
919-968-7877

lystrabooks@gmail.com
www.lystrabooks.com

Printed in the United States of America

LYSTRA BOOKS
& Literary Services

Praise for *The Christmas Redemption*

In *The Christmas Redemption,* **Landis Wade spreads a bounty of presents under the reader's Christmas tree.** Whether you are young with a facile imagination about the activities of North Pole elves, or have a liking for real life courtroom drama, complete with skillful, zealous lawyers facing a judge with his mind already set, or whether you like action stories with quick, quirky plot twists, you will enjoy this hilarious Christmas tale. You also will find answers to long-held questions such as why naughty kids get lumps of coal.

The story reminds us that those things which are most real and meaningful in our lives—e.g. love, courage, forgiveness—are never seen in the abstract; and that the experience of unseen things is what make us True Believers in the goodness, peace and joy we celebrate at Christmas.

- Don Carroll author of *The Beguines and the Search for Visionary Consciousness; King Arthur and the Consciousness Gene;* and *The Consciousness Trilogy*

The Reindeer Hoverboard is supposed to fly, which makes it the most popular Christmas gift in the past 50 years. But it carries a warning that says it only works for True Believers. It's up to the husband and wife legal team of Thad Raker and Sarah Kennedy to defend the lawsuit brought against Tip Top Toy Company, who made the hoverboard.

This charming courtroom drama weaves a dour judge, colorful personalities and the magic of Christmas in one tale. Intricacies of North Pole politics and little-known details about Santa and his family come to light in this entertaining story for young and old. Readers will delight in the surprising, multi-layered plot and cleverly-drawn characters, and their hearts will be warmed.

— Ann Campanella, author of
Motherhood: Lost and Found

The Christmas Redemption could only have been written by an experienced attorney who understands the power and traps of legal proceedings, and who can create and solve complex, human puzzles.

This is a drama of serious courtroom competition, Christmas fantasy, and international issues. The weaving of these forces is brilliantly done.

— Jack Hemphill, author of
Exhibition of the Song Bo Paintings;
Redbriar; and *The Ridge Walker*

"Believing without seeing." It's a powerful idea, and it's at the heart of *The Christmas Redemption*.

There are many books and movies on the subject of Christmas. Enough so that you might think there's nothing new to say, that every story has been told. You'd be wrong, though. Landis Wade has concocted an entertaining, well-paced and very readable Christmas story. It has a villain, a mysterious central character, a well-crafted plot, and a happy ending. Read this book and remind yourself how much fun it is to read a good story.

— Ralph Peeples, Professor of Law,
Wake Forest University.

It's John Grisham meets Santa Claus, for a hoverboard ride that seamlessly blends courtroom drama, corruption, climate change and Christmas with great humor—and with a message about the true meaning of Christmas and the importance of family.

A fast and funny read, full of legal laughs and Christmas chaos, Landis Wade makes a True Believer out of me, in the magic of the holiday season!

- Tracy Curtis, humorist and author of
Holidazed; *Beach Bummed;* and *Trophy Mom*

With intelligence, a jurist's wit, and his usual panache, Landis Wade's latest yuletide saga evokes the magic of *Miracle on 34th Street* in a lawsuit by Santa skeptics against a toy company making Reindeer Hoverboards that only fly for True Believers. The implications soon become global, and lawyer Thad Raker and his daughter, Liz, fight to save the future of Christmas—and the planet—from the effects of an international conspiracy.

At once clever, heartfelt, and engaging, *The Christmas Redemption* is a merry legal adventure that is perfect for holiday reading.

- Phillip Lewis, author of *The Barrowfields*

For True Believers, everywhere

Also by Landis Wade

The Christmas Heist: A Courtroom Adventure

The Legally Binding Christmas: A Courtroom Adventure

Visit the author's website,
www.landiswade.com

Visit the Facebook page,
www.facebook.com/thechristmasheist

THE CHRISTMAS REDEMPTION:

A Courtroom Adventure

by

Landis Wade

[signature]

LYSTRA BOOKS
& Literary Services
Chapel Hill, NC

"I wear the chain I forged in life," replied the Ghost. "I made it link by link, and yard by yard; I girded it on of my own free will, and of my own free will I wore it."

Charles Dickens, A Christmas Carol

Friday, October 5th

A blunt object pressed against Hank Snow's back and nudged him forward, toward a one-story building with a large sign that read, "County Jail."

Snow turned around and looked up at the heavyset officer who'd placed a baton between his shoulder blades. "Do you mind?"

"Move it," the officer said.

Snow's hands were behind his back, linked together by handcuffs. He was a short man, half the size of his captor. The baton jabbed him in the neck and Snow grumbled as he picked up the pace.

1

The officer shoved Snow through the front door, down a narrow hall and into a side room. He grabbed and lifted a resistant Snow onto a metal folding chair and took a seat at a laminate desk across from Snow. Slapping at his shirt pocket, the officer grabbed a pen.

"Full name and occupation?" the officer asked.

"Hank Snow. Toy manufacturer."

"Employer?"

"North Pole Enterprises."

"Never heard of it."

Snow looked at the officer's nameplate and put his photographic memory to work. Officer Terry Stanback made the Naughty list as a 6-year-old and never improved.

"I'm sure my company has a record of you somewhere," Snow said.

Officer Stanback looked up from his paperwork with a raised brow but didn't respond. He uncuffed Snow, pressed Snow's fingers on an ink pad and took his prints.

A few minutes later, Snow was in a cell that was small even for his stature. Solid plaster walls surrounded him. One had a small window set high that allowed a ray of light to fall to the floor. He sat on the lone bench in the cell and stared at the locked steel door. Of all the jails in the world, he found himself in the one in Thad Raker's hometown.

He thought about what had gone wrong. The intelligence for his mission was sound. He'd had a good plan and 99 percent of it had gone well. Number 10 Downing Street in London: No problem. The Élysée Palace in Paris: A breeze. The Hofburg Imperial Palace in Austria: Elementary. That's the way it had been with the official residences of heads of state throughout the world. He was able to slip in, get the building's security blueprints and get out without being caught. That is, until he arrived at the White House, where he found a document unlike any he'd seen. It had nothing to do with the security of the White House and everything to do with the security of the North Pole. He'd immediately photographed it and sent it by encrypted email to Zachary Cane, vice chairman of the Elf High Council.

Within four hours after Snow left the White House, he was on the run from the law, a publicized fugitive. Somehow, the government learned of the break-in, obtained Snow's picture and plastered it everywhere, along with a description: small man, eyes as black as coal.

The longer Snow thought about the manhunt that led to his arrest, the more certain he was that he'd been betrayed. Only the members of the Elf High Council knew his schedule and assignment. It must have been one of them.

Snow's thoughts were interrupted when the metal door swung open and Officer Stanback was back. "Get up. You have a visitor."

The officer cuffed Snow and escorted him from his cell to a small interview room. He started to lock Snow's handcuffs to the metal table in the center of the room when he was interrupted.

"It's all right," the woman in the room said. "We'll be fine."

Officer Stanback looked at her and shrugged. "I'll be outside if you need me."

Snow kicked a wooden chair from under the table with his right foot, placed his shackled hands on the open side of the chair and used his elbows and legs to pull himself up. With legs dangling, he swiveled his torso to face the woman who'd taken a seat across the table.

"Good afternoon, Mr. Snow," she said.

Snow said nothing. She looked familiar and he tried to place her.

"Do you remember me?" she asked. "I'm Sarah Kennedy. I was one of the lawyers who represented the county in the Twirly Masters trial 11 years ago."

"I remember. You quit the case before it was over

and married Thad Raker, the lawyer on the other side. Not very committed to your work, are you? I see you're alone. Did you quit on Raker, too?"

Sarah laughed. "No, I haven't quit on my husband. We're happily married and we practice law together. He couldn't be here because he has a deposition today. You might find the case interesting. It involves a toy called the Reindeer Hoverboard."

Snow knew about the Reindeer Hoverboard but he didn't let on that he did. He was also familiar with the manufacturer, Tip Top Toy Company.

"Why are you here?" Snow asked.

"A friend of yours called the office this morning and asked us to help you."

"What friend?"

"Snowflake."

That made sense to him. Snowflake was a member of the Elf High Council and the most likely Council member to want to help him. She'd always been friendly to him, even when he opposed her in Council decisions. He suspected she knew his family secret but she'd never admitted it. And he'd never asked.

But why Raker and his wife would want to represent him, that was a puzzle. He'd caused nothing but trouble for them in past court cases.

"You're facing serious charges and the possibility of a long prison sentence," Sarah said. "You need a lawyer."

Snow knew the charges against him were serious but he didn't want the kind of publicity that came with Thad Raker's courtroom trials. There were facts about the North Pole he had no intention of disclosing, ever, for any reason.

"My freedom is not the important thing here."

"Snowflake thinks it is. She wants to help you."

Snow thought about the danger to the North Pole revealed in the White House document. His criminal case was secondary. It was time to end this conversation. "You think sending me lawyers who despise me is helpful? It's not," he said.

"I don't know you well enough to despise you."

"Your husband does."

"It's true he doesn't like you," Sarah said. "You lied in court and interfered with his efforts to save Christmas. But he trusts Snowflake and he is a man with an open mind. Remember, he's Thad Raker, a True Believer."

Snow kept his stern demeanor but smiled inwardly as he recalled how Raker had come to believe in Santa Claus during the Henry Edmonds trial. "Believing in Santa Claus is not the same thing as believing in me."

"You sound like you're giving up," Sarah said. "This doesn't sound like the Hank Snow I remember. That Hank Snow wouldn't back away from a fight."

"You can tell Raker the good news. He won't have to represent me. I plan to plead guilty. I can do that on my own."

Same Day – Lunchtime

Augustus Langhorne Stark, judge retired, sat at a corner table in the local diner, listening to the "order-up" calls of the cooks and the clanging of dishes and silverware, thinking about how the present had swallowed his past. He missed his days as a young lawyer and his long career as a judge. He truly loved the law, felt alive in the courtroom and enjoyed the challenge of an interesting case. Now those days were gone, in the past, like his lovely wife, Kay. Only memories remained. Good ones, but memories nonetheless, leaving him sad and uncertain about what to do with himself each day.

The melancholy that absorbed Judge Stark's thoughts vanished when a young woman walked through the front door and waved to him. Liz Raker's smile and youthful enthusiasm had a cathartic effect on the judge's mood. The two had met for lunch every Friday since she graduated from college five months earlier.

"Hello, Liz," he said. "Pull up a chair."

Liz sat down and reached for the glass of iced tea Judge Stark had ordered for her. "Thanks, judge. How was your week?"

"Same as usual. Big things. Important things."

Liz laughed.

"And you?" Judge Stark asked. "Anything exciting happen for you this week?"

Liz smiled and her eyes brightened. "As a matter of fact, it did."

"Do tell."

"I got a job," Liz said. "Well, actually, it's an internship, with a small stipend, plus room and board, but it's in my field of study and it's important work. I leave in 10 days."

"Save the planet kind of work?" Judge Stark asked. He was proud of her for graduating with honors in environmental science.

Liz smiled. "Yes, and I'm going to Greenland to do it."

"Greenland? You'll have to take an early flight every Friday to make our weekly lunches." Judge Stark laughed to conceal his disappointment.

"I know," Liz said. "I'm going to miss seeing you, but we can talk regularly. I'll teach you how to use Skype."

Judge Stark had no idea what a Skype was. "What does your dad think about you running off to Greenland?"

"He's been quiet about it. I think he was hoping, like you, that I would take the LSAT this fall and go to law school next year, but I reminded him that my help at the law firm after graduation was just temporary, until I found the right job."

"Well, I'm sure he's as proud of you as I am."

Liz reached across the table and squeezed Judge Stark's hand. "Thank you."

The waitress brought two plates to the table and refilled their tea glasses. "I ordered the usual for you," Judge Stark said.

As Liz dug into her food, Judge Stark thought about the last 11 years. Liz was now 22, but she was still a True Believer, like her father. After helping her dad win the Twirly Masters trial as an 11-year-old, Liz formed the Band of True Believers, a group of Santa Claus believers who pledged to save

Christmas should the need arise. The BTB hadn't met since Liz went to college and there'd been no Christmas threats requiring its services, but the mere thought of the BTB put Judge Stark in a good mood and he started to hum one of his favorite Christmas tunes.

"I recognize that song," Liz said. "Don't you think it's a little early for Santa Claus to be coming to town?" They both laughed.

"Tell me how you landed your internship," Judge Stark said.

"You remember the event I helped organize in Washington, D.C., last summer?"

"How could I forget? With the rise in sea level, it was dubbed the 'Slosh on Washington.' You had more than 100,000 protestors on the National Mall."

"We did," Liz said. "A recruiter heard me speak that day and called, saying he liked my message. He offered me the internship with his client."

"What is it?"

"It's a toy company headquartered in Nuuk, but it owns some land in the northern part of Greenland that could be threatened by rising temperatures."

As Judge Stark mulled over the idea of Liz leaving, Liz added, "Did you hear about the new case Sarah and Dad have been working on the past few months?"

"I don't believe I have," he said.

"It has to do with a hoverboard that won't fly," Liz said. "Not only that, it's called the Reindeer Hoverboard."

"Nice name. Was it designed to be a Christmas present?" Judge Stark asked.

"Yes. Lots of people bought the hoverboard last Christmas. Dad and Sarah represent the manufacturer and it's a big case. I joked with Dad about this being his third chance to save Christmas, but he didn't think I was funny."

"You never know about these things, Liz. Your dad has a way of attracting cases where Christmas is on trial. He would be wise to keep an open mind."

"Good point," Liz said. "I'll remind him before I leave for Greenland." She stopped talking to look at the television on the wall overhead.

"What is it?" Judge Stark asked.

She frowned and shook her head. "I know that name."

Judge Stark turned around to see the caption below the broadcaster's face that read, "Hank Snow arrested for White House break-in." He called to the waitress, "Can you turn that up?"

The reporter said Snow was being held in the county jail for prosecution by the local U.S. attorney.

That meant he'd be on trial in front of federal judge J. P. Lake. Judge Stark knew J. P. Lake well.

When Judge Stark turned back, Liz said, "When I was 11, Hank Snow cornered Holly and me and stole a document from us that Dad needed in the Twirly Masters trial. I hoped I would never see him again."

"How is your elf friend?" Judge Stark hoped to calm Liz.

"She's fine. Picking fights with the North Pole establishment, for good causes." Liz paused. "Why do you think Hank Snow broke into the White House? And how do you think he ended up in jail here?"

"Who knows," Judge Stark said. "The man has a way of getting into trouble around here about every 10 years. It usually has something to do with Christmas."

Same Day – 2:30 p.m.

The first few months of the Reindeer Hoverboard lawsuit taught Raker three things about Tarina Winter, the president of Tip Top Toy Company, his new client. She was headstrong, mysterious and uncompromising. Her behavior today in her deposition was no exception.

The court reporter eyed Tarina, ready to take down exactly what she said, but Tarina was silent in response to the last question. The reporter glanced at Raker, but he could only shrug.

"Did you understand my question?" Robert Greenback was the lawyer for the plaintiffs. Victims, he liked to call them.

"I understood it," Tarina replied.

"Well?" Greenback was impatient. "Is the answer yes or no?"

"It's not that simple."

"And why not?"

"Because answering your question does not answer why the hoverboard didn't work."

Greenback was a big man. When he stood up to get water from the credenza, it was all effort, with a bit of wheezing. He poured a glass, took a swallow and turned to the court reporter. "Read back the last question."

The court reporter complied. "Was Tip Top Toy Company the manufacturer of the computer chip that caused the Reindeer Hoverboard to malfunction?"

Tarina Winter still didn't speak.

Greenback sat back down. "I will break it down for you. Was Tip Top Toy Company the manufacturer of the computer chip?"

"Yes."

"And did the computer chip control the flying abilities of the Reindeer Hoverboard?"

"Yes."

"And did the Reindeer Hoverboard, the most sought-after Christmas present in the last 50 years, turn out to be a complete disaster?"

"Objection," Raker said. "Argumentative."

Greenback puffed his chest. "Mr. Raker, this is cross-examination. Of course, it's argumentative. Your client is the one being difficult."

"Mr. Greenback, this is not closing argument. The objection is to the form of your question, in particular, the words 'complete disaster.' Please rephrase your question."

"You don't think it was a complete disaster, just a disaster?"

"I'm not the one testifying," Raker said.

"I couldn't agree more," Greenback said.

Raker didn't enjoy this part of the legal process. Defending a deposition was like having a cavity filled without Novocain. All he could do was grunt—object—when the dentist-like lawyer struck his nerve.

Tarina Winter appeared unmoved by the bickering among the lawyers. Her facial expression could best be described as confident but indifferent. She looked to be in her 60s, a tall, fit, well-shaped woman, with porcelain skin complemented by silver-gray hair. She brushed a fallen strand of that

hair from in front of ice-green eyes and stared at
Greenback. "I am fully prepared to answer your
question, even though it is ill-conceived,
presumptuous and sarcastic."

Robert Greenback became more aggressive.
"Insulting me is not a good idea."

"I'm sworn to tell the truth, Mr. Greenback."

"That's the way you want to play it?"

"I'm not here to play with you, sir. I can see you
are not a very playful person."

Raker made a note on his legal pad that said,
"Remind client to be respectful," and then circled it.

Greenback tossed a notepad onto the table.
"We'll come back to this topic later. Tell me about
your company. It will come in handy when I get the
judgment that puts you out of business."

Tarina Winter ignored the jab. "What do you
want to know?" she asked.

"For starters, who owns it?"

"I have a 50-50 partner."

"His name?"

"Next question," Tarina said. "One that has
something to do with this lawsuit."

Greenback slammed his fist on the table, causing
Raker's papers to scatter and the water in his glass
to swirl. He shouted at Raker. "Do we have to go to
the judge about this behavior?"

Raker remained calm, picked up his glass and took a sip of water. "Perhaps we should. I can let the judge know you lost your temper and tried to break my table. On the other hand, it would be quicker if you just laid a foundation for your question."

"Fine," Greenback said. "Ms. Winter, was your partner involved in overseeing the manufacture of the computer chip?"

"No."

"You're not going to tell me his name?"

"No. And it's not a he. Honestly, what makes men think that two women can't own a successful business?"

Greenback didn't apologize. "Let's focus on the business itself. Headquarters?"

"Greenland."

"Manufacturing plants?"

"U.S., U.K., Italy and Argentina."

"Where was the computer chip made?"

"Greenland."

"Who designed the chip?"

"You're looking at her."

"Now we're getting somewhere," Greenback said.

Tarina Winter brushed some lint from her sweater. "It took you long enough."

Greenback leaned back. "Are you always this difficult?"

"Not always. But when my time is taken up by men like you who spend their time blaming others for a chance to get a large fee, then yes, I can prove to be difficult."

"Are you saying your company is not at fault for the failure of the hoverboard to fly?"

"Yes."

"Can you prove it?"

"Mr. Greenback, I've watched enough courtroom television to know that the proving part belongs to you."

"You're an arrogant woman."

"Aren't we a match."

"Fine," Greenback said. "We'll do this slowly, one fingernail at a time. The Reindeer Hoverboard failed to fly for 75 percent of the adults who bought it, correct?"

"That's true. For those 75 percent."

"Whose fault was it?"

"Theirs."

"I don't understand."

"I didn't expect you would."

Greenback eyed Tarina Winter with jaw-clenched contempt. "Why was it their fault?"

"They didn't heed the warning label."

Greenback took out a document, marked it as Exhibit 1, and laid it in front of the witness. "This is the warning label. Would you mind reading it into the record?"

"Not at all." Winter took out her glasses, placed them on her nose and tucked the stems over her ears. Then she read, "Warning: This product only works for True Believers."

"How did my clients ignore the warning label?" Greenback asked.

"Come now, Mr. Greenback, you can figure this out."

He picked up the exhibit and looked closely at the warning label. "What exactly is a True Believer?"

"Ah! That's the best question you've asked today." She turned to Thad Raker. "Mr. Raker, would you like to tell him?"

Greenback was impatient. "What's she talking about?"

Raker swallowed a smile and looked Greenback in the eye. "A True Believer is an adult who believes in Santa Claus."

Silence.

"Is this some kind of joke?"

"I'm not joking," Raker said.

Greenback looked back at Tarina Winter. "Are you telling me this case has something to do with whether my clients believe in Santa Claus?"

Tarina Winter sat up straight and brushed another strand of silver-gray hair away from her left eye. "Welcome to my world, Mr. Greenback."

*Saturday, October 6th*

Judge Stark sat in the same room at the same table where Sarah Kennedy had met with Hank Snow. This morning, like every morning since Kay's death, Judge Stark had awakened to an empty house, fed his dog and fetched his newspaper. An article written by reporter Austin Land caught his attention right away. It was about Hank Snow's arrest. Land was the lawyer-turned-reporter who'd helped Raker in the two Christmas trials in Judge Stark's courtroom.

The headline read: "President of International Toy Company Arrested." The sub-headline read: "White House Document Stolen."

The article reported on the mystery of the crime and the man. It laid out facts that would cause readers to wonder why someone associated with a toy company would have an interest in government secrets. It also discussed the details of Snow's role in the Christmas trials that made Thad Raker a local Christmas celebrity.

Judge Stark finished the article while he drank his morning coffee and then reflected. There was something about Hank Snow that never made sense. He smiled when he made the decision to go to the jail.

Officer Stanback brought Snow in and shackled him to the table. "I'll be right outside if you need me, your honor."

When the two were alone, Judge Stark said, "Thank you for meeting with me."

"I didn't have any choice."

"True. Being a retired judge has its perks. Being a prisoner has few."

Snow pulled at his wrists and the cuffs clanked.

"Nothing I could do about that," Judge Stark said. "Since I don't represent you, they aren't going to take any chances. Wouldn't look good for a former judge to get hurt in their jail."

"Why are you here?" Snow was hostile.

Judge Stark laughed. The man did have spunk. He liked that. "You know, Mr. Snow, I find you an enigma. Curious. Puzzling. Not truthful, based on your testimony in my courtroom, but with a certain passion that harbors unrevealed motives. You're a man running an important enterprise, but unwilling to admit it."

"And that's why you're here? To study me?"

"Not exactly. I'm here to help you. The state made me retire as a judge, but I still have my law license."

"Things must be slow for lawyers in this town. First, Sarah Kennedy. Now, you. Is there a long line outside?"

Judge Stark smiled. "You need a lawyer. I need something to do. Based on what I've seen of your past performances in court, this case won't be boring."

"I don't need a lawyer. I'm going to plead guilty."

"Interesting. Mr. Snow, that intrigues me even more. So yes, I will be your lawyer."

Snow had a contemplative look on his face. When he finally did speak, he said, "I have a question about the attorney-client privilege."

"What do you want to know?"

"If you are my lawyer, does that mean that whatever I tell you, you will keep to yourself and not share with anyone else without my permission?"

"As long as you don't tell me you are about to commit a crime, then yes, I will keep your secrets."

"You won't tell anyone, including Thad Raker and his new client?"

Judge Stark wondered where this was going. "Are Raker and his new client tied up in this?"

"Just answer my question."

This was going to be more interesting than he thought. "Of course, Mr. Snow. Your secrets will be safe with me, even from Raker and his new client, whoever that is."

"One final thing," Snow said. "Will you help me plead guilty, not try to talk me out of it?"

Judge Stark leaned back. "Why? Are you guilty?"

"Doesn't matter. Just answer the question."

"I draw the line at being a potted plant. I will let you know if you should fight the charges. But if you don't accept that advice, I will help you plead guilty."

Hank Snow stretched his right hand as far as he could before his manacle caught it. Judge Stark took it in his right hand. "You're hired," Snow said. "What now?"

"You tell me the truth, not those yarns you spun in my courtroom."

"What do you want to know?"

"Mr. Snow, every story has a beginning, a middle and an end. I would like you to start at the beginning and work your way forward from there."

For the next two hours, Snow talked and Judge Stark listened. When Officer Stanback interrupted and said their time was up, Judge Stark knew he'd picked the perfect case to bring him out of retirement.

Thursday, October 11th

Holly sat on a hallway bench on the first floor of the North Pole's administrative building, waiting for her latest complaint to be heard by the National Elf Relations Board. This time, the case concerned water leakage in seven of the nine North Pole departments. She knew she'd have her work cut out for her. The NERB was a stodgy bunch of commissioners. The chief commissioner was the worst.

In her official job, Holly was Snowflake's right-hand elf, the junior archivist who recorded and preserved Santa's gift-giving history for all the world's children and kept track of all the True

Believers. It was an important job but not her only job. She also held the post of union representative, which kept her busy filing complaints on behalf of elves in different departments.

The door to the NERB hearing room opened and the bailiff announced her case. Holly stepped in, took off her ball cap and approached a bench occupied by three elves. She walked up and stood 10 feet from the bench.

"We don't have all day," the chief commissioner said. "What's this about water in the work areas?"

"Sir, this is a battle we've been fighting for years."

The chief commissioner looked at a pile of papers to his left. "Yes, you've filed 50 complaints on this issue in the past five years."

"It's worse now," Holly said. "The little fixes you've authorized in the past are not going to address the real problem."

The elf with a rat face and spiky hair sitting next to the chief commissioner leaned forward. "And what, may I ask, is the real problem?"

Holly had done her research. She took out a hand-held device, pushed a button and pointed it at one of the walls. The elves on the panel turned to look. A map of the North Pole region came into view.

The North Pole ice sheet was in the center of the map, surrounded by water and lands farther out. Greenland was the closest of any size.

The chief commissioner looked at his watch. "We appreciate the geography lesson, but what does this have to do with water leaking into the work areas?"

Holly used a laser pointer. "This was the North Pole ice sheet 50 years ago." Holly pushed a button on her device and the image changed. "Notice the same area 20 years ago." She pushed the button again. Another image appeared. "And this is the ice sheet earlier this year. Do you notice anything different about these images?"

The three elves on the NERB whispered to one another. The chief commissioner then turned his attention to Holly.

"You are out of order, young elf. Your hypothesis is—"

"My what?" Holly could barely contain herself. "This is not a theory."

The chief commissioner reached for a book to his right and flipped to the first page. He ran his finger down the index and, finding what he was looking for, turned to the page. "Here it is," he said. "Elf High Council Edict 1983 states that there is no such thing as global warming and all further research on the subject is banned."

Holly pointed at the screen with the forefingers of both her hands. "Climate change is real. The ice is melting and if you don't do something soon, we'll be under water and out of business. What then for Christmas?"

The chief commissioner slammed his gavel on the bench. "Enough!"

All six eyes glared at Holly. Dark eyes. None friendly.

"I suggest you destroy your images, return to your duties and say nothing of your complaint to any of your fellow elves. You don't want the Elf High Council to find out about this. You could be banished for spreading these rumors."

Holly took a deep breath and didn't speak. She'd have to figure another way to solve this problem.

"And another thing," the chief commissioner said. "It's about time you toss your blue jeans, tennis shoes and baseball cap, and start dressing like the rest of the elves."

Holly turned and walked from the room. Bunch of demented elves. Couldn't find their way out of a stocking that was open at both ends.

County Court

Honorable
Judge Johnson

Friday, October 12th

The motion hearing in the hoverboard case was scheduled to begin at 9:30 a.m., so Raker, in his usual style, planned to be there 15 minutes early. He met Tarina Winter at his office beforehand to explain the reason for the hearing.

"The court will rule on Greenback's request to certify this case as a class action."

"What class?"

"All the adults for whom the hoverboard failed to work."

31

Raker had a question he should have asked sooner of the woman who designed a hoverboard to fly only for True Believers. "Do you have some kind of relationship with Santa Claus?"

Tarina Winter diverted her eyes from Raker and looked out his office window. "Relationship? No. I wouldn't say I have a relationship."

Raker looked at the clock and saw that it was time to leave for court. He would have to pick up this topic later.

On their walk to the courthouse, Tarina Winter said nothing. Not even a comment about the nice weather. They came to a newsstand that displayed a newspaper with another front-page article about Hank Snow, written by Austin Land. Tarina stopped and bought a copy while Raker waited.

When they arrived in the courtroom, the clerk handed Raker an amended calendar.

"What's changed?" Raker asked. The clerk pointed at the judge's name. It read, "Cleve R. Johnson, Judge Presiding." Raker felt his heart race.

Eleven years earlier, Raker battled Johnson in the Twirly Masters trial. The good news was that Raker won and the judge held Johnson in contempt of court. The bad news was that in the years that followed, Johnson had gone out of his way to make trouble for Raker. Now, freshly elected to the judiciary, Cleve R. Johnson was the Honorable, and Raker knew this was not true. More concerning, this was Johnson's first case as a judge.

"All rise," the bailiff said, at which point the side door opened and Judge Johnson walked in. He had a lumbering step as he made his way up to and behind the bench, where he stood for a moment and looked around the courtroom. His frown turned to a Grinch-like smile when he and Raker made eye contact.

"Announce yourselves for the record," Judge Johnson said.

"Robert Greenback, counsel for the victims."

"Thad Raker, counsel for Tip Top Toy Company. Sarah Kennedy will be working on the case, too, but she's attending to another matter this morning."

"This has to be your worst nightmare, Mr. Raker, being in my courtroom," Judge Johnson said.

Raker didn't take the bait. When Johnson finished glaring at Raker, he turned to Greenback. "You've filed a motion to certify this case as a class action. Proceed."

Greenback grabbed two large piles of paper from the desk in front of him and asked to approach the bench. He dropped one set on the corner of Raker's desk and handed the other set to Judge Johnson.

"What's this?" Judge Johnson asked.

"These," Greenback said, "are the papers proving without a doubt that this product liability case should be certified as a class action."

"Is there a common set of facts among all potential class members?"

"Yes, sir."

"Are they seeking personal injury damages?"

"No, sir."

"They all want the same relief?"

"Yes, their money back and punitive damages for the fraud perpetrated on them."

"How many people?"

"Approximately 100,000."

"What do they have in common?"

Greenback looked at Raker and smiled. "Would you like to tell him?"

"Tell me what?" Judge Johnson focused on Raker.

Raker knew there was no ducking the issue, but he could use it to make a point. "The plaintiffs are adults who do not believe in Santa Claus. That is what they have in common. It's a fact critical to my client's defense."

Judge Johnson placed his hands on the bench and leaned forward. "I thought you were a fool in our case 11 years ago. Your days of playing Santa's helper are over. You mention him in this courtroom and you do so at your peril. Do I make myself clear?"

"Are you saying that if the evidence supports my client's defense, you won't allow it?" Raker felt the judicial forces of nonbelief trying to suffocate him.

Tarina Winter blurted out, "That's exactly what he's saying."

Johnson looked at Tarina. "Stand when you address the court."

Tarina locked eyes with Judge Johnson. Raker leaned over and whispered to her to get on her feet, but she didn't move. "I assume," she said, "that standing is a sign of respect. Well, I don't respect you."

Judge Johnson's face was getting red. "Ms., Ms.—"

"The name is Tarina Winter, president of Tip Top Toy Company, the defendant in this case. And you, sir, are a nonbeliever who intends to deny me my day in court."

"Not true. You will get your day in court."

"I don't see how that's possible. You just told my lawyer that he can't mention Santa Claus in this case."

"This case has nothing to do with Santa Claus."

"So, you're prejudging the case. Is that how the law works here?"

Raker looked at Tarina in disbelief. He wondered if she had any idea the damage she was doing to her case.

"Do you realize, Ms. Winter, that I can hold you in contempt of court right now?"

"Mr. Johnson, I have no doubt that a man with the power to tell people what they can and cannot believe has the power to do just about anything. I never thought believing in Santa Claus would put me in jail."

Johnson looked around and said, "Mr. Greenback, your motion is granted."

Greenback handed Raker a copy of a proposed order and handed the original to Judge Johnson. Raker scanned it. It defined the class of plaintiffs as adults who purchased a Reindeer Hoverboard who do not believe in Santa Claus. It appointed Martin Stubble, the lead plaintiff, as class representative. Judge Johnson read it, signed it and thrust it back at Greenback.

"Mr. Raker," Judge Johnson said. "I might as well have signed an order that said the class of plaintiffs consists of adults who bought a Reindeer Hoverboard who breathe oxygen." Raker chose not to respond.

When Greenback returned to his seat, he shook Martin Stubble's hand and patted him on the shoulder. Stubble, a thin man of 35 years, looked at Raker through wire-frame glasses that rested on an elongated nose. Dressed in a suit that sagged in all the wrong places, he didn't look like a man who would buy or ride a hoverboard.

"Where do the parties stand on completing discovery in this case?" Judge Johnson asked.

Greenback explained that he'd taken Tarina Winter's deposition and the parties were working together to exchange documents and schedule other depositions.

"I want this case on a fast track," Judge Johnson said. "The parties have two months from today to complete discovery and then I'm going to hear a motion from plaintiffs to hold defendant liable as a matter of law. Given what I've heard, this case won't make it to a jury trial because, if the defense is based solely on the existence of Santa Claus, I will dispose of the case myself."

"Thank you, your honor," Greenback said.

"And one more thing. I'm ordering a psychiatric examination of Ms. Winter to occur in the next two weeks. Set it up."

Monday, October 15ᵗʰ

Liz Raker's plane touched down at the Nuuk airport and she made her way through customs. She had done her homework and knew that Nuuk was the largest city on the biggest island in the world that's not a continent, but smallest among all capital cities in the world by population. In a country made mostly of ice.

If asked, she could recite plenty of facts about the place. The Greenland ice sheet was 1,500 miles long and 680 miles wide near its northern margin. Though the measurements change from year to year, the ice sheet was more than a mile thick, on average, and up to two miles at its thickest. Enormous glaciers and ice caps decorated the island's periphery. A changing climate was bearing down on all of it.

When Liz collected her bag, she was surprised to find a friend there to meet her.

"Hello, Liz," Twirly Masters said. "My, my. You are one smart-looking environmental science graduate. Yes, you are!"

"Twirly, what are you doing here?"

He pointed to someone walking toward them. "Keeping him out of trouble."

Liz dropped her bag and ran toward Henry Edmonds. She wrapped her arms around his chest and snuggled her head to his right shoulder. Edmonds laughed and returned the hug. "Hello, Liz. It's good to see you, too."

When Liz and Henry released each other, Twirly said, "Your ride's this way."

"Wait. Why are you picking me up? Why are you even in Greenland? Do you know about my internship?

"Let's catch our ride first," Twirly said.

When they were in their taxi, Twirly Masters started talking, as he was apt to do.

"We're helping a manufacturing arm of Santa's enterprise that's tip-top, for sure," Twirly said. "The company needs your expertise on a top-secret project, and you're just the person for the job. Yes, indeed. We don't know much. It's strictly need-to-know stuff. But you'll have the details soon enough."

Liz knew this was a short speech for Twirly. She first met him as an 11-year-old when her dad represented Twirly in a jury trial to prevent his property from being taken by the county. The case had to do with Santa's distribution system. By saving Twirly's property, her dad saved Christmas. Liz never doubted again.

Henry Edmonds said little on the ride. He was a big man with a quiet disposition. She met him during Twirly's trial but she'd heard about him for years from her dad's bedtime story, and knew that his first name was her middle name. He was the brave man her father represented in what was known as the Trial of the Century one year before she was born. The case had to do with the Naughty and Nice lists. The two men made a good team. Liz was glad to have them with her.

When Twirly was through telling Liz what little he knew, he began to bring her up to date on everything he'd done since they were last together.

Liz half listened, and used the remaining time in the cab ride to take in the rugged landscape that swept by her window. She could see blue ripples on a large bay, acting as a mirror for the west facing slope of a rugged mountain. The peaks were covered with dashes of snow and ice. Liz breathed in the beauty.

Thirty minutes after they left the airport, the taxi pulled up to the top of a hill and parked. Everyone got out. The view made Liz stop and stare.

"It's the Nupp Kangerlua fjord," Twirly said. "Just spectacular, don't you think?"

Half a mile in the distance was a corridor of the bluest, purest water Liz had ever seen. Barren hills climbed from the water's edge on the far side. On the downward slope in front of her was a collection of small houses painted in an assortment of bright colors. Red. Green. Blue. Yellow. Like supersized Monopoly houses laid out on a hillside, with a front yard full of crystal blue water and floating ice.

"Yes," she said. "Spectacular."

They walked down a steep path to a house perched above the water. "Your home for the next few months," Twirly said.

When Liz entered the front door, she saw a woman sitting at a rolltop desk, studying a map. A lock of silver-gray hair covered her left eye. She wore a long butterscotch dress made of thick cloth, with a hood that fell behind her neck.

"Liz," Henry said, "this is Tarina Winter, president of your new employer."

"Nice to meet you," Liz said. "Thank you for hiring me."

"I didn't. I got an anonymous call that you were coming."

"I don't understand."

"Your benefactor must be someone who cares about the future of Christmas."

Liz was confused. She thought about the top-secret project Twirly mentioned. "I'm here to study the melting of the Greenland ice sheet. What does that have to do with the future of Christmas?"

"You're a bit like your father," Tarina said. "Always asking questions."

"How do you know my father?"

"He's representing my company in a case that will make or break the company and affect the future of Christmas. We're depending on him."

Liz thought about the materials forwarded to her by the recruiter. Her internship was with TTTC, LLC, and she didn't recall any of her dad's clients by that name.

"It's the hoverboard case," Tarina said.

And then Liz put it together. "Your company is Tip Top Toy Company?"

"One and the same."

Tarina walked over, put her hands on Liz's shoulders and said in a low but direct voice, "If we're going to save Christmas for generations to come, we're going to need your help, too."

Tuesday, October 23rd

It was a regular weekday morning at the Kennedy & Raker law office, with lots of calls from would-be clients looking for that magical legal touch. Raker was on the phone with one such caller when he heard the melody of the front-door chime. Tarina Winter must have arrived.

"Yes, sir," Raker said, "I know your case is important to you, but we don't handle lawsuits against the Easter Bunny. What's that? No, not the Tooth Fairy, either."

Raker held the phone away from his ear as the caller's voice grew louder. "So much for being a full-service law firm," the man shouted. Raker referred the caller to one of his least favorite adversaries, hung up the phone and hurried to collect his client.

Tarina Winter stood in the foyer in a knee-length white dress that flared at the waist. Two-inch heels highlighted her athletic legs. She had an impatient frown on her face and held a banker's box of files.

"Let me help you with that," Raker said. He reached for the box, but she walked past him to the conference room and dropped it on the table. When he entered the room, she was seated at the table. He looked at the box.

"It's all there," she said. "Though I don't know why it's needed."

"It's called discovery. Each side is entitled to see relevant documents that belong to the other side." Raker grabbed several files from the box. One was labeled "Chip Design" and another was labeled "Ownership." He flipped through one, then the other, and saw that lines had been redacted with a black marker.

"You've marked out the name of your co-owner and the name of the person who designed the hoverboard computer chip?"

"Yes."

"Why?"

"It's none of their business who owns the company with me and I already admitted that I designed the chip."

"But—"

"You know my defense and this information has nothing to do with it."

The melody of the door chime sounded again, and soon thereafter, Sarah Kennedy joined Raker and Tarina in the conference room. "Sorry I'm late," she said. "What did I miss?"

"Your husband was criticizing me for keeping secrets," Tarina said.

Raker exchanged looks with Sarah, who smiled and said, "Don't take it personally. He's just trying to be helpful. By the way, how was your flight?"

"Other than the lack of legroom and the food they tried to pass off as chicken, it was fine," Tarina said. She turned to Raker. "Liz wanted me to tell you, she likes working for my company."

"I was planning to speak with you about that. Liz called to give me the news and was excited about the coincidence. Is that what it is, Tarina? A coincidence?"

"I'd love to chat about my company's work, Thad, but shouldn't we be focused on my lawsuit?"

Raker looked at Sarah, who came to his rescue. "I'm curious," Sarah said. "Why did you design a hoverboard that works only for True Believers?"

"Not my idea."

"Whose idea was it?"

"Doesn't matter." Tarina Winter brushed some lint from her white dress and looked back at her lawyers. "How's the case going?" she asked.

"I'm preparing for Martin Stubble's deposition," Sarah said. "It's this Friday. I'd like you to be there to look him in the eye. It might keep him honest."

"Can't do it," Tarina said. "I'm only in town for a short visit. I have to get back to Greenland."

Raker pulled out his phone to look at his calendar. "Your medical examination is set for 10 in the morning. I hope you plan to stay for that." He heard the frustration in his voice.

"Yes, I'll be there, but I have a question. If I say I believe in Santa Claus, the doctor will tell Judge Johnson that I'm crazy. What do you want me to do?"

"Just listen to the doctor's questions and tell the truth," Raker said. "We'll deal with the doctor."

Sarah agreed. "If you're asked, you can't deny the existence of Santa Claus," she said, "or you will have no case."

"About your case," Raker said, "there is another strategy to consider. My gut tells me that you didn't design the chip, and if I'm right, you could let the party at fault take the blame and save your company."

Winter stood up. "No."

"Can you say why not?" Raker asked.

"I can, but I won't."

Raker had a thought. "Did Santa Claus design the chip that propels the Reindeer Hoverboard? Are you trying to protect him?"

"Good guess, but no."

"You realize," Raker said, "that Judge Johnson could strike the True Believer defense as inadmissible fantasy and award judgment to plaintiffs, bankrupting your company."

Tarina smiled. "It's time you remembered who you are, Thad, and what you're capable of doing. You saved Christmas twice before."

"What does this case have to do with saving Christmas?"

Tarina moved close to Raker, placed her right hand on his left arm and leaned toward him. "Thad, this case has everything to do with saving Christmas. All you have to do is win."

"But how can I do that if you won't tell me the facts?"

"Concentrate on belief. It's belief that counts. Remember that, and we'll win this case."

Tarina left the room. When the front door closed, Sarah said to Raker, "It's a good thing we're True Believers."

Wednesday, October 24th

The medical office was in a redbrick building near a strip mall. The sign on the front door read, "Dr. A. J. Wright." Tarina Winter looked at the sign and scowled. "We shall see about that," she said to Raker, who stood beside her.

They entered a small lobby and a receptionist handed Tarina some forms to fill out. Tarina immediately handed them back. "I'm not a patient. I won't be filling out any forms. I'm only here because the court ordered me to be here."

The receptionist looked surprised but didn't argue. "The nurse will be right with you."

When Tarina and Raker were about to take their seats, a woman entered the room. "You must be Tarina Winter," the woman said. "I'm Dr. Wright's nurse."

"And what kind of doctor is Dr. Wright?" Winter asked.

"Excuse me?"

"Psychologist or psychiatrist?"

"She's a psychiatrist, well-versed in personality disorders, and experienced in mental assessments."

"A certified quack," Tarina said to Raker, loud enough to be heard by the nurse.

The nurse started to respond but Raker spoke first. "I'm Ms. Winter's lawyer and—"

She cut him off. "Lawyers aren't permitted in the examining room. You can read Dr. Wright's report when she's done." She looked at Tarina. "Follow me."

Before Raker could respond, Tarina touched his elbow. "It's fine. I don't need a lawyer for this. I've dealt with plenty of nonbelievers."

Tarina followed the nurse into a small examining room. It had a table against one wall, a chair in the corner, a rolling chair with a round seat and a cabinet unit that included a counter stacked with medical books and supplies. Tarina threw her coat on the padded table and sat in the chair in the corner. The nurse took her blood pressure, 115 over 65, and left the room.

A few minutes later, there was a knock on the door. A woman in her late 40s entered. She wore a white lab coat, buttoned up to her chin. She had a small beak of a nose, a narrow face and accusing eyes. It looked like her mental patients had worn all compassion from her countenance. She put out her hand. "I'm Dr. Wright."

Tarina nodded, but didn't shake.

"I realize," the doctor said, "that this is a court-ordered medical examination and you are an unwilling patient."

"I'm not your patient at all. But I'm here. So, let's get on with it."

The door opened and the nurse re-entered, carrying a notepad. "I've asked my nurse to be in the room as a witness. You understand."

"Of course, I do. It's okay. I don't trust you, either."

Dr. Wright turned to her nurse and said, "Paranoia." The nurse checked a box.

"Do you mind if we start with your childhood?"

"Yes."

The doctor turned to the nurse. "Combative." The nurse checked another box.

Tarina could see where this was headed. She looked at the nurse. "Why don't you go ahead and check 'nut job who believes in Santa' and we can get this over with."

Dr. Wright intervened. "Ms. Winter, since you've gotten to the heart of the issue, tell me this. When did you first start believing in Santa Claus?"

"I believed in his work from the beginning."

"Not his work. Him."

Tarina thought about Santa. "After my dad died, Santa was hard to accept."

"Oh," the doctor said, "you had a traumatic experience?" The doctor pointed to a box on the form the nurse held and the nurse checked it off.

Tarina knew they would never believe the truth. How her mother was an elf who fell in love and broke tradition by marrying an adventuresome though mere mortal. How her father was a Viking explorer. How her childhood was full of excitement, growing up in Greenland in a time long, long ago. How, years later, after her father died, her mother met and married the man everyone called Santa. And how Santa did nothing to prevent Tarina's banishment from the North Pole. "It was traumatic. I never wanted Santa to be my father."

The doctor grabbed the form from the nurse and made a notation. "Let me get this straight," the doctor said. "You believe that Santa Claus is your father."

"No. I didn't say that."

"I'm lost."

"I expected as much before I got here today." Tarina checked her watch. She was ready for this examination to be over. The truth was the best way to do it. "My mother is Mrs. Claus."

For a full 30 seconds, the room was quiet. The doctor sat on the rolling chair. She rolled it close to Tarina, leaned in and said, "We can help you, Ms. Winter."

Tarina stood up. "I'll be going now. I believe you have enough to write your report." She walked out the door and down the hall to the lobby. When she entered the lobby, Raker was looking at his cellphone. She tapped him on the shoulder as she walked by and went out the front door. Raker caught up to her on the sidewalk.

"How did it go?" he asked.

"I'm afraid I've made your job a lot more difficult."

Thursday, October 25th

Holly was hard at work in The Archives' basement, her jeans rolled up to her knees, gathering documents to move to the first floor. Despite her efforts over the last five years to convert the old scrolls and manuscripts to electronic format, there were still thousands of written materials to protect. She was cold, exhausted and frustrated from working in icy water that covered her ankles.

The ice sheet upon which Santa's village sat was supposed to be a mile thick. That was the official word from the Elf High Council. But it wasn't true, and Holly knew it. When she started doing research on the Internet to fact-check the Council's propaganda, the Council learned about it and passed an edict in a 4-to-1 vote prohibiting investigation of unproven theories. The Council considered the effects of global warming on the North Pole to be one such theory.

What blocked research couldn't reveal, a melting ice pack could. After her hearing before the NERB, Holly discovered water entering The Archives' basement and reported it to Snowflake, the one member of the Elf High Council who believed that Santa's village was at risk. Holly also confided in some progressive young elves, and together, they conducted a variety of secret core drilling experiments. Some were done in department basements. Others were done on the perimeter of the village. What they found shocked them. The ice sheet was only 20 feet thick at best and five feet at worst. Seawater was rising through fissures in the ice. As the ice became more unstable, there was the risk that the weight of the buildings would cause them to collapse into the Arctic Ocean.

That's why Holly was so hard at work gathering important records in The Archives' basement, and why she was so tired now. She had worked for several hours when she sat down on a bench to rest and get her feet out of the water. That was when she noticed a large book on top of the stack to her right. The words "Village History" appeared on the cover. Holly was curious. She grabbed the book and opened it.

A family tree was in the front of the book. She scanned the page until something caught her attention. She didn't think what she read could be accurate, but that's what it said. Mrs. Claus had been married before.

Entries on the family tree were indexed to pages in the book. Holly flipped to the page about Mrs. Claus' first marriage. It told the tale of a Viking explorer who made a home in Greenland and won the love of Mrs. Claus. They had one child, a girl. Her name was Tarina.

She turned back to the first page and looked to the bottom of the family tree where it showed the union of Santa and Mrs. Claus. There was a line from their names to a name below, the name of a child, but the child's name had been scratched out. Holly looked for the corresponding page in the book but it had been torn out.

Holly ran up the steps and found Snowflake at work in The Archives' computer room.

"Did you know that Mrs. Claus was married before she knew Santa?" Holly held out the book.

"Of course. I'm the keeper of The Archives, and that book is under my care."

"Is it a secret?"

"Not to Santa and Mrs. Claus."

"But to others?"

"I don't believe they publicized it."

"But you knew?"

"I know lots of things, Holly."

Holly was miffed. "What about the child from the first marriage?"

"What about her?"

"I've never heard Mrs. Claus talk about her," Holly said. "Did something happen?"

Snowflake shut down her computer, and gave Holly her attention. "Yes, Holly, something did happen. After Tarina's father died, Mrs. Claus met Santa. As you would expect, he was the perfect gentleman. He treated Tarina like his own child and brought her into the family business."

"What happened to her?"

"It's not for me to tell," Snowflake said. "It's not my story."

Holly thought about pressuring Snowflake to tell her the story, but then remembered she had another mystery to solve. "The family tree makes it look like Santa and Mrs. Claus had a child, but the records are incomplete." She pointed to the scratched-out name in the family tree and the missing page in the back.

"Yes," Snowflake said. "I know about this."

"Was it vandalism?"

"No. It was protection. I did it as a favor."

"Wait," Holly said. "You're required to maintain records, not destroy them."

"In this situation, it had to be done. Until today, there were only a few people, counting me, who knew that Santa has an heir."

Holly was surprised. "Does the child have a name?"

"Not my story to tell," Snowflake repeated. "Now, I have something you should see." She reached under the counter, pulled out a thick spiral-bound manual and handed it to Holly. It had strange acronyms on the cover: "SOP of SRP."

"Go ahead. Open it," Snowflake said.

Holly opened the book to learn that "SOP" meant "Standard Operating Procedure" and "SRP" meant "Santa Relocation Plan." The Standard Operating Procedure for the Santa Relocation Plan.

"I don't understand," Holly said.

"I got the idea for the plan from a Greenpeace initiative called the Santa Relocation Project. The organizers of the project felt that if they could get children to believe that Santa's village was sinking due to global warming, the children would stir their parents into action to save the planet."

"That was a great idea."

"It was just marketing," Snowflake said. "The Greenpeace environmentalists were not True Believers. They believed in a healthier planet, not in Santa Claus. But it made me realize we needed a plan if we have to leave. That's why I put this manual together."

Holly gripped the thick manual. "What do you want me to do?"

"Do what you do best. Take charge."

Friday, October 26th

Sarah Kennedy sat next to the court reporter in Robert Greenback's law office, organizing her notes for the deposition of Martin Stubble, the plaintiffs' class representative in the hoverboard lawsuit. Raker was at the law library doing research for the case and Tarina was in Greenland.

Greenback entered the room with Stubble in tow. He parked his client in the seat across from Sarah and got down to the business of obstruction. "Before we get started," he said, "I will not tolerate questions about Santa Claus. I'm sure I have an ally in Judge Johnson. Are we clear?"

Sarah decided not to acknowledge his bullying. "Swear the witness, please," she said to the court reporter.

Martin Stubble raised his right hand and took the oath. His perspiration was evident from the damp circles at the armpits of his shirt. Sarah had no plan to make him feel less nervous.

"Mr. Stubble," she said, "as your lawyer probably explained to you, I will ask you questions and the court reporter will transcribe your answers. Your testimony can be used in court. Used against you. Is that clear?"

Stubble nodded affirmatively.

"Also, your lawyer may object from time to time, but he can't interfere with you answering my questions."

"Now, wait a minute," Greenback complained.

"Mr. Greenback, as you know, the procedural rules are clear. If you instruct him not to answer factual questions, I will file a motion to have you sanctioned. Despite Judge Johnson's disdain for Santa Claus, the law is on my side."

"You can't tell me what to do," Greenback said.

"You're right, but I can tell you what I will do. If Judge Johnson ignores the law, I will appeal, and you will be on the hook for all the fees and expenses of your obstruction and we will be right back here, with an order requiring your client to answer my questions."

Before Greenback could respond, Sarah looked at Stubble and launched her first question. "Why did you buy the Reindeer Hoverboard, Mr. Stubble?"

"Well, I—" Stubble searched for an answer. "I thought it would be fun."

"And was it?"

"No."

"Why not?"

Stubble laughed nervously. "It didn't work."

"Why not?"

"It just—" Stubble looked to his lawyer.

"Mr. Stubble," Sarah said, "your lawyer is not here to answer the questions. That is your job."

"I don't understand why you are asking me why it didn't work. How am I supposed to know that?"

"Can you read?"

"I can."

"Did you read the warnings? On the box? On the hoverboard itself? In the written directions inside the box?"

"You mean the thing about being a True Believer for it to work?"

"That's exactly what I mean."

"Yeah, I read it in all three places, but it didn't make any sense to me."

"Does it now?"

"I understand it's about needing to believe in Santa Claus for the thing to work."

"Do you believe in Santa Claus?"

"Objection," Greenback said. "Irrelevant."

"Your objection is noted for the record," Sarah said. Looking at Stubble, she said, "You can answer the question."

"Are you kidding me?"

"Not at all," Sarah said. "Do you believe in Santa Claus?"

Stubble looked around as if to find a hidden video camera. Finally, he looked at Sarah again. "You really want to know if I believe in Santa Claus?"

"I do." Sarah waited.

"Ms. Kennedy, I'm 35 years old. No, I do not believe in Santa Claus."

"Then you got what you paid for, didn't you?"

"What?"

"You bought a hoverboard that only works for adults who believe in Santa Claus. You got what you paid for, right?"

"This is a scam. I bought a hoverboard that doesn't work."

"Have you asked an adult who believes in Santa Claus to try it out?"

"Well, I—"

Greenback jumped in. "You mean like you or your husband?"

Sarah ignored him. "Mr. Stubble, would you agree that if the hoverboard you bought were to work for an adult who believes in Santa Claus, it is not defective?"

"But it won't—"

"I'm not asking you for your opinion. I'm simply asking you to admit that if it does work for a True Believer, it's not defective."

Stubble studied the question. Sarah maintained eye contact.

"I suppose," Stubble said, "that if there is an adult in this world who believes in Santa Claus and my hoverboard works for him, then yes, it is not defective."

"And if your hoverboard is not defective, you have no claim against Tip Top Toy Company, right?"

"Yes, if the hoverboard works, I have no claim. But I know it doesn't work."

"For you, right?"

"Right."

"A person who, by his own admission, does not believe in Santa Claus."

"True."

"Thank you, Mr. Stubble. Now let's talk about the alleged harm done to you and the other plaintiffs. You weren't hurt on the hoverboard, were you, Mr. Stubble?"

"No. It never got off the ground."

"And you've been in touch with the other plaintiffs, haven't you? Conducted an online survey, correct?"

"I did."

"And none of the 100,000 plaintiffs were hurt, were they?"

"It's hard to get hurt when the thing doesn't move."

"No one was hurt, were they?"

"No."

Sarah closed in on the finish. "Your lawyer wants the court to award you and the plaintiffs punitive damages, correct?"

"Absolutely."

"Is it your contention that promoting belief in Santa Claus constitutes willful, wanton and malicious conduct that should be punished?"

"Of course."

Sarah grabbed a file and pulled out a picture of two children sitting on Santa's lap. "Are these your twin girls when they were in first grade?"

Stubble looked startled. He glanced at the picture and nodded.

"Mr. Stubble. What did you tell your girls that year about Santa Claus?"

Stubble's demeanor suggested he was trapped. Greenback objected, but Sarah didn't let up. "You can answer, Mr. Stubble."

"I told them that if they didn't believe in Santa, they wouldn't get any presents. But it doesn't—"

"So, you led them to believe that Santa is real?"

"Sure. They were kids."

"Do you see anything willful, wanton or malicious about that?"

"Of course not."

"So, it's okay to lie to children, just not to adults who like to file lawsuits?"

"Well, no. I mean—"

"Do you think you should be punished for doing it?"

"That's different."

Sarah pushed back her chair. "Mr. Stubble, how is it that my client should be punished for telling a discerning adult like yourself that Santa is real while you escape punishment for misleading young girls on the topic? Isn't that a double standard?"

Stubble looked at Greenback and then back at Sarah. "I never really thought about it."

"Perhaps you should, Mr. Stubble. That's all the questions I have."

Tuesday, October 30th

Holly was updating the True Believer list in The Archives building when she heard a knock at the door. When she opened it, Zachary Cane, vice chairman of the Elf High Council, and two of his supporters pushed past her to come in.

"Holly, I have a warrant for your arrest." He handed her a piece of paper.

"What's this about?" Holly asked.

"You know what you've done," Cane said. "Clandestine research. Drilling without a license. Stirring up lies about the environment. It's all in the warrant."

"You're lying to everyone at the North Pole. Global warming is science, not a political idea."

"Watch your tongue," one of the elves said.

"He's right," Cane agreed. "You have enough problems without adding a charge of disobedience."

"Is that what you call trying to save Christmas? Disobedience?"

"Enough!" Cane was seething. "Your court date is in mid-December. Until then, I suggest you keep your mouth shut. Let's go."

Cane and his underlings escorted Holly to the detention center and dropped her off. The jailer told her she could make one phone call. She thought about calling Snowflake but then she had another idea. She dialed a number and Liz Raker answered on the first ring.

"Liz, it's me, Holly."

"Holly! Great to hear from you. How's everything at the North Pole?"

"That's why I'm calling."

Holly first met Liz when Liz was an 11-year-old ready to give up her belief in Santa Claus. Thad Raker was representing Twirly Masters at the time and Holly was an elf-in-training living at Twirly's house. The girl and the elf became fast friends. Holly knew she could count on Liz.

For the next few minutes, Holly updated Liz on the instability of the ice pack that was home to Santa's village.

"That's terrible," Liz said.

"Yes," Holly said, "it means that if something isn't done soon, Christmas as we know it will cease to exist."

Liz was silent on the other end. "And there's one more thing," Holly said. "I need your help. The cartel of Neanderthals who run this place just arrested me for telling the truth. I can pick a representative for my trial. I pick you."

"But I'm not a lawyer," Liz said.

"Don't have to be," Holly said. "You know the science and you're smart. The hearing is in December."

After Holly spent one night at the detention center, an obese elf with a pock-marked face escorted her to a two-story building. The covered entrance was supported by two columns wrapped in garland made of sparkly tinsel. The sign above the front doors said, "Naughty or Nice Justice Center."

She and her escort entered an open foyer and took the wide stairs in front of them to the second floor, where they arrived at the entrance to the Elf High Council's chamber. Holly took off her hat and held it in her hand as she walked inside and down the aisle.

The Elf High Council members sat behind a high bench, with Zachary Cane at the center. He was taller than the other elves. His black, stringy hair was parted in the middle and pulled behind pointy ears; it spilled onto his sloped shoulders, looking as if it hadn't been brushed in days. His face showed anything but Christmas cheer.

The Council was made up of five members but only four elves looked down at Holly, one of whom was Snowflake. The chairman, Hank Snow, was not present. It was clear that in his absence, Zachary Cane was in control.

"You petitioned to be released from detention pending your trial. Take a seat." Cane pointed to a chair to Holly's right.

"Where's the chairman?" Holly stood where she was. "Where is Mr. Hank Snow?"

"That is none of your concern."

"I know the rules. I'm entitled to a hearing before the entire Elf High Council. You don't have jurisdiction to charge me, hold me or convict me, without Hank Snow being present."

Cane ignored Snowflake, who sat to his left, and conferred with the two male elves to his right. They nodded in response to what appeared to be Cane's suggestion.

"Mr. Snow has not reported in to the North Pole for several months," Cane said. "Therefore, the Council is exercising the edict of ascension. The Council's work will not be delayed. Henceforth, I will be chairman and we will operate with four members, not five. Now, let's—"

Snowflake interrupted. "Please note for the record, sir, that the vote is 3-to-1 on that edict. I vote against it." Holly smiled. At least Snowflake was on her side.

Cane grunted. "No matter. The edict stands." He turned to Holly. "It shouldn't take long to return you to detention, where you belong. What do you have to say for yourself?"

Snowflake spoke up. "Holly is not a flight risk, sir. Besides, the penalty for the crime in question is banishment. If she leaves, it just saves you the trouble. As a Council member, I have the right to have her released into my custody until the trial. I hereby exercise that right."

"Very well." Cane looked down at Holly. "You'd better be on your best behavior until the trial or I will add to the charges against you. You're free to go, until the trial."

Thursday, November 1st

Raker and Sarah were leaving their law office at the end of the work day when Raker got the call. "Thad, it's Augustus Stark. Do you and Sarah have time to drop by for a little chat?"

"Judge Stark, it's great to hear your voice. How about lunch tomorrow?"

"It's about Hank Snow and that new case you've got representing Tip Top Toy Company."

This caught Raker's attention. "We'll be there in 15 minutes."

Judge Stark welcomed his guests and offered them a drink. Sarah accepted a glass of wine. Raker settled for a glass of water. Better to have his wits about him when having a conversation about Hank Snow.

When everyone was seated in the den, Judge Stark said, "I bet you're wondering why I asked you to drop by."

"The name Hank Snow got my attention," Raker said. "He disrupted two of my most important trials. When I heard his name in the same sentence with the hoverboard case, I wondered how he might be involved. Is there something we should know?"

"As a matter of fact, there is. Problem is," Judge Stark said, "I can't tell you."

"I don't understand," Sarah said.

"Attorney-client privilege."

"What? You're representing Hank Snow?" Raker asked.

"Yes." Judge Stark's face had a big smile. "For about a month now. Does that make your day?"

While Raker was trying to absorb this news, Sarah said, "Judge, when I met with Hank Snow, he didn't say he knew anything about Tip Top Toy Company. Is he going to help the plaintiffs?"

"That's why I asked you to drop by," Judge Stark said. "Snow received a subpoena from Greenback to testify in the case. Snow wants me to move to quash it."

Raker slid back on the sofa. "I'm guessing that if Judge Johnson makes him testify, Snow will hurt our case and that's the reason for this friendly warning."

Judge Stark deflected. "What do you know about your client?"

"Not as much as we'd like to know," Raker said. "Our client appears more interested in beliefs than facts. I'm a True Believer, too, but Sarah and I need something to work with in court."

Sarah leaned toward Judge Stark. "Why are you representing Hank Snow? He lied in your courtroom in two trials, a violation of your rules of court."

"Criminal defendants are entitled to an attorney. That's the first reason. The second reason is my newest rule: Retired judges should not have to die of boredom."

"You're going to defend him, just to avoid being bored?" Sarah asked.

"Should help pass the time."

"Well, forgive me if I don't wish you success," Raker said. "I can't pull for a guy who has a history of trying to sabotage my efforts to save Christmas."

While Raker was driving home, Sarah looked at her phone and saw an email with some news. "We received a filing today in the hoverboard case."

"What's Greenback up to now?" Raker asked.

"It's not Greenback. Some group called the League of Informed Entrepreneurs, otherwise known as LIE. They filed a motion to intervene in the case."

"The league of what? And why do they want to become a party to this lawsuit?"

Sarah took a moment to do an Internet search.

"According to their website, they are a nonprofit consortium of businesses who despise Santa Claus."

"I don't understand."

"Neither do I, but you will have to handle the hearing because it's next Wednesday, and I'm meeting with witnesses to sign affidavits that day."

"Any other news?"

Sarah scrolled through the "About" section of LIE's website.

"Yes," Sarah said. "Hank Snow is listed as a board member."

Wednesday, November 7th

Court was supposed to begin at 9:30, but the judge was nowhere to be seen. His tardiness reminded Raker of the Twirly Masters trial where Judge Stark confiscated Johnson's Rolex watch for being 15 minutes late to court. Those were the days.

While he waited, Raker noticed that Greenback was engaged in conversation at counsel table with a well-dressed man and woman. They must be with the League of Informed Entrepreneurs. Allies in the fight against his client.

"All rise," the bailiff shouted. Raker checked his watch. It was 10 a.m.

Judge Johnson walked in the side door but was in no hurry. He stopped by the clerk's desk and scanned the room. Eye contact with Raker was not friendly. The judge spoke with the clerk, grabbed a file and walked up the two steps to his bench, dropping the file with a loud thump on the bench before him. Placing his hands behind his back, he waited for the bailiff to read him in. When the oyez speech was done, Johnson remained standing.

"Why are we here, Mr. Greenback?"

"Three matters, your honor. One, we have the report from Tarina Winter's psychiatric examination."

"Hand it up," Johnson said. "I've been looking forward to this."

As Greenback approached the bench, Judge Johnson looked at Raker. "Where is your client, Mr. Raker?"

"She's attending to business in Greenland, your honor."

"She must not think this case is very important."

"To the contrary, your honor."

"Doesn't matter," Johnson said. "Case may not last that long anyway." He reached over and accepted the medical report from Greenback and sat down.

For the next five minutes, activity in the courtroom was on pause as Johnson buried his nose in Dr. Wright's report. Raker could hear mutterings from Judge Johnson. He thought he heard him say "fascinating" several times and he was sure he heard the judge snicker twice. When Johnson put the report down, it appeared as if his spirits had been lifted.

"What's item Number 2, Mr. Greenback?"

"Your honor, we served a subpoena on a witness who refuses to testify."

Before Johnson could respond, the main door to the courtroom opened. Raker turned to see Judge Augustus Langhorne Stark walk in. He was dressed in a light gray suit, the perfect match for his thinning hair, and he sported a red tie. Ten strides later, he was seated in a pew on Raker's side of the courtroom. An old man, to be sure, but the confidence was there despite the absence of his black robe.

Raker turned back around and looked to the bench. Judge Johnson's mouth was open, as if he had choked on a piece of fruitcake and couldn't get air. His eyes darted from Judge Stark to Raker and then to Greenback.

"You were saying, Mr. Greenback, that a witness has refused to testify."

Raker heard a voice behind him say, "That must be my client, your honor. If it please the court, I will enter my appearance. Augustus Stark, counsel for Hank Snow. Mr. Snow objects to Mr. Greenback's subpoena."

"You're supposed to be retired," Johnson said. "What are you doing in my courtroom?" with emphasis on the word "my."

"I have gone into private practice, your honor. Looks like we've swapped places."

"Yes," Johnson said. "I make the rules now, not you."

"Suits me. I understand one of your rules is starting court 30 minutes late. That should give me a little more time to sleep in."

Johnson looked around on his desk for his gavel. When he found it, he picked it up and swung it hard. To Raker's surprise, it slipped from Johnson's hand and flew backward into the portrait of a recently deceased and well-respected state Supreme Court justice. The gavel went through the jurist's head, leaving a hole where his face should have been, and a dangling handle for all to see.

"Better to use short motions," Judge Stark said, "like this." He cocked his elbow at a 90-degree angle and showed Johnson how to hammer a nail into a piece of wood.

Johnson's face reddened. "I need no instruction from you. This is my courtroom, and don't you forget it."

"Not a problem. Every time I come in here and see the Honorable up there with a gavel between his teeth, it will be easy to remember."

"Stop it. I can hold you in contempt," Judge Johnson shouted.

Raker watched for Judge Stark's response. "Judge Johnson, I'm here to represent my client. I intend to show you all the respect you deserve."

There was no doubt in Raker's mind: Judge Stark was in control.

Judge Johnson turned back to Greenback. "You may be heard."

"Thank you, your honor." As Greenback reached for the document in front of him, Judge Stark passed the bar that separates the lawyers from the spectators and took a seat beside Raker.

"We have a motion to compel Hank Snow's testimony," Greenback said. "May I approach?" Johnson granted permission and Greenback handed the document to Judge Johnson, who took a few minutes to read it. When he was done, he looked at Judge Stark.

"Why is your client refusing to testify in this matter?"

"He says he doesn't want to," Judge Stark said.

"You know very well that is not a good reason. If you were in my seat, you would hold him in contempt."

"I told him the same thing." Judge Stark reached into his front pocket and pulled out a note. "He told me to read this to you. It says, 'Go jump in a glacial lake. I'm already in jail.'"

This was the second time Judge Johnson's authority had been called into question since Judge Stark entered the courtroom. Johnson was agitated.

"Why is this man important to your case, Mr. Greenback?"

Raker perked up. He was curious to know the same thing.

"He is chairman of an international toy company called North Pole Enterprises. He's an expert in the toy business and can offer testimony on the standard of care with respect to warning labels. He's also done business with Tip Top Toy Company and has relevant factual information."

"Wait a minute," Judge Johnson said. "That name sounds familiar. Is he—?"

"One and the same," Judge Stark said. "From the trial you lost to Raker 11 years ago."

Raker always wondered how much Johnson knew about Snow's conspiracy with the county, Johnson's client in the Twirly Masters trial. Raker watched for Johnson to reveal the truth, but he didn't.

"Tell you what I'm going to do," Johnson said. "I can't send Snow to jail, but I can bring him to my courtroom. Mr. Greenback, you can take his testimony, here, with me presiding. Mr. Raker, you'll get your chance to cross-examine. As I recall, you don't care much for the man."

Judge Stark got up, patted Raker on the shoulder and whispered, "Good luck, Thad. Might be the most interesting case you've had yet." He walked down the aisle and out the door.

Johnson was becoming impatient. "Anything else, Mr. Greenback?"

"A third party's motion to intervene."

"Someone else wants to be a party in this case?" Johnson didn't look happy.

"I'd like to introduce Tammy Brighthouse, attorney for the League of Informed Entrepreneurs."

The woman who stood up was the one Greenback had been speaking with before the hearing began. She was in her middle 40s and wore a dark blue pantsuit with light red pinstripes. Her long brunet hair was pulled back from her face with a clip on the top of her head and it fell to the middle of the back of her shoulders. She had a long, accusing face, like she'd never been happy about anything.

"Ms. Brighthouse, why does your client want to get into this case?"

"LIE plays an important role in commerce," she said. Raker was glad she used the acronym. The more times the court heard it, the better he felt.

"How so?"

"Truth drives business. Without business, the economy doesn't work."

"What does that have to do with this case?"

"We understand that Tip Top Toy Company intends to try to prove Santa Claus is real."

"Not if I can help it." Johnson looked at Raker as he said it.

"In any event, the result of promoting the Santa lie is devastating to business. We want to stop it. We're seeking an injunction against Tip Top Toy Company. No more lies about Santa."

"Go on." Johnson was more conciliatory now.

"LIE received a grant 20 years ago to study the harm caused to retail businesses when parents lie to their children about Santa Claus.

"There's harm in it to businesses?" Johnson appeared to be warming up to Tammy Brighthouse.

"Yes, but worse. It's also harmful to children."

Johnson gave the lawyer his full attention. "I'm listening."

"We've done a lot of work in the field. Interviews. Studies. Medical examinations of children. Stress tests on retail businesses in the years after children stop believing. It all points to a detrimental impact on the mental development of children and the bottom lines of retail businesses. We want to be able to present our findings in this case."

Johnson looked at Raker. "What do you have to say about this?"

"We oppose the motion for LIE to become a party in this case."

"Why?"

"LIE doesn't have standing to be a party. They have not—"

Tammy Brighthouse interrupted. "We anticipated this argument, your honor, but we do have a stake in this case." She reached under the desk and grabbed a tote bag that looked like it might hold a snowboard. She unzipped the bag and pulled out a four-by-two-foot object. It was flat, about two inches thick, and had rounded corners. The surface was white, with streaks of red.

"This, your honor, is a Reindeer Hoverboard." She laid it on the floor between her and Raker, facing Judge Johnson. Then she stepped on it.

"What are you doing?" Johnson asked.

"Nothing at all," she said. "That's the point, your honor. This is LIE's Reindeer Hoverboard, bought and paid for, yet it doesn't work. We have a claim, too."

Raker jumped in. "Your honor, this doesn't prove anything other than the fact that Ms. Brighthouse doesn't believe in Santa Claus."

"Ha," Brighthouse snapped back. "Everything about you, Mr. Raker, is Santa Claus this and Santa Claus that. You're on LIE's top-ten list of false promoters."

"Your honor," Raker said, "LIE is just another purchaser. Its interest can be represented by Mr. Greenback, the attorney for the plaintiffs."

"We opted out of the class. We want to represent ourselves."

"Then they should file their own lawsuit," Raker said.

"We thought about that," Brighthouse replied. "I have the lawsuit ready to file today." She held up a stack of paper. "Wouldn't it make sense, your honor, to have one lawsuit instead of two? It would save time and expense. And I can promise you that we have relevant information that will impact this case."

Greenback stepped forward. "Your honor, if it please the court, plaintiffs do not object to working with LIE on this case."

"Ms. Brighthouse," Judge Johnson said, "I don't plan to delay this case just because you're joining the party. We're on a fast track. Is that understood?"

"Yes, sir," she said. "We can help move this case along."

"Good. Anything else, Mr. Raker?" Judge Johnson asked.

Raker knew he was beaten. "No, sir."

"Motion is allowed," Johnson said. "LIE is officially in the case. Prepare an order for me to sign, Ms. Brighthouse. May your presence in this case bring an end to the Santa drama in this courtroom."

Johnson slid the motion papers to the side and asked the clerk for his calendar. After studying it, he said, "On Tuesday, December 18th, I will hold the dispositive motion hearing. You can bring deposition transcripts and affidavits with you and we'll hear live testimony from the doctor, your clients and Mr. Snow. I'll set aside two days."

"Your honor," Raker argued, "we've asked for a jury trial."

"I know what you've asked for, Mr. Raker. The hearing will determine whether or not you get it. If the facts are undisputed, I will decide this case. Am I understood?"

Raker remembered what his law professors said about lawsuits, "You have your good days and your bad days. It's a marathon not a sprint. Best to jog on."

"Yes, sir," Raker said. He would return to fight another day.

Thursday, November 8th

Liz was up at daybreak with a warm cup of cocoa, sitting in a comfortable chair by the large window in Tarina Winter's house. She was watching the morning light dance off the fjord when Tarina came in the room. "Good morning, Liz. Did you sleep well?"

"I did, thank you."

"You've been working hard the last four weeks. Have you read all the reports?"

"Yes, and I've done some research on my own."

"What do you think?"

Liz put down her mug and walked to the large map of Greenland on the wall. She grabbed the pointer and placed the tip in the map's northwest corner. "Here's Thule Air Force Base," she said. She slid the pointer to the east a few inches. "And here's the location of Camp Century." Sliding the pointer to the northeast, she said, "According to the reports, this is the location you've chosen."

"Do you think it's a good location?" Tarina asked.

"If nothing is done to slow global warming, it will suffer the same fate as the North Pole. It's just a matter of time."

"What's a matter of time, Liz?" Twirly asked, entering the room with Henry Edmonds. They both looked at Liz as she pointed at the map on the wall.

"Go ahead," Tarina said. "Tell them what you know."

"Thule Air Base is the U.S. Air Force's northernmost facility, 750 miles north of the Arctic Circle and 550 miles east of the North Magnetic Pole." Liz explained that the Air Force base got its start as a location to defend Danish colonies on Greenland from German aggression in World War II. From there, it morphed into a prime NATO location during the Cold War. Camp Century, 150 miles to the east, was the location the U.S used to launch Project Iceworm.

"Project Iceworm?" Henry asked.

"Yes," Liz said. "An ill-conceived plan to hide 600 nuclear ballistic missiles in several miles of tunnels below the surface of the ice to defend against a Soviet airstrike." The U.S. built the tunnels, she explained, which included underground barracks, shops, hospitals and churches, but then core samples revealed that within years the ceilings would collapse due to the glacier shifting. "The U.S. government abandoned the site," Liz said.

"We should all sit," Tarina said. "There are things Twirly and Henry need to know before you go on."

When they all found chairs, Tarina began. "About 20 years ago, Project Iceworm became declassified. At the time I read about it, I was concerned that global warming would eventually destroy Santa's village. Project Iceworm gave me an idea and I started planning for the worst. I took out loans to build an underground village, similar to Camp Century but not as wide or as deep, and in a different part of Greenland, a remote area where I thought the ice sheet was more stable. I've asked Liz to study the scientific data we've collected. She was about to tell me what she thought when you walked in."

"Wait a minute," Henry said. "There's an underground village in Greenland where Santa can move if necessary?"

"We're finishing construction. It will be larger than the village at the North Pole," Tarina said.

"Well, imagine that," Twirly said. "It's downright ingenious! Santa's village: From 'iceberg' to 'ice tunnel'." Twirly and Henry laughed.

Tarina looked at Liz with concern on her face. "What do you think, Liz? Will it last?"

"The problem with an ice sheet is that it's firm on top but constantly moving underneath, spreading outward, with the rise and fall of temperature. This can cause tunnel walls to expand and retract and ceilings to collapse. That's the risk."

"What does your gut tell you?" Tarina asked.

Liz looked at the map on the wall. "I like the location, but I need to finish my review of all your data and study the core sample reports."

"Everything you need is at our toy plant on the south side of Nuuk," Tarina said. "We can make that happen."

"I also have a few suggestions for your engineers," Liz said.

"You can continue your work at the plant. We have a room devoted to the Santa Relocation Plan with a video feed to our construction team on site."

"Nice name," Liz said. "I like it."

"What else will you need?" Tarina asked.

"After the construction is complete, I would like to inspect the tunnels for any hint that the ice is shifting," Liz said. "My suggestions to your engineers could add a few weeks to the construction schedule."

"That should put the completion date at mid-December," Tarina said.

"Based on what Holly said about the North Pole, that may cut it close," Liz said.

"Maybe Santa should just move to Miami," Twirly joked.

Everyone laughed but Liz. "Not a good long-term plan. If the politicians don't do something to contain global warming, the icebergs around here will flood the beaches down there. Either way, Santa gets his feet wet."

"Well then, we'd better get to work," Tarina said. "I will be back and forth over the next month to help the lawyers work on the hoverboard lawsuit, so the three of you need to manage when I'm gone. There's a young elf at the plant who will assist you. Her name is Mistletoe."

As everyone got up from the table, Liz put her hand on Tarina's forearm. "You never told me what's at stake in the court case."

"Everything, Liz. To build the village, I mortgaged the plant and the land where the underground village is located. If I lose the case, my lender will take everything."

"Wait, that means—"

"Yes, there's nowhere for Santa to go."

"We have another problem, too," Twirly added. "Tip Top Toy Company produces 50 percent of the toys Santa makes and has the added responsibility of being the brain center for Santa's distribution grid, yes, indeed! So, if Tip Top goes out of business—"

"If it does," Henry said, "half the world's population won't see Christmas for many years to come."

Friday, November 9th

Hank Snow was cuffed at the wrists and ankles and transported by police van to the federal courthouse, where two federal marshals met and signed for him. They led him inside and down a long corridor, where they placed him in an interview room. One wall was half-covered by a mirror. Snow suspected it had see-through glass on the other side. They could watch and question him all they wanted. He wasn't going to play along.

A tall man in a dark suit entered the room and flashed his identification card. FBI. Judge Stark stepped in behind him and took a seat next to Snow.

"I'm FBI Agent Lemming," the man said. He looked sullen. Snow had dealt his whole life with a man with that look: Zachary Cane.

"We know what you took," Agent Lemming said, "and the U.S. government wants it back."

Snow wasn't going to give him the satisfaction of an answer. Better to wait on his lawyer to respond.

"What is it you think my client took?" Judge Stark said.

"He knows." A finger pointed at Snow's face. Accusing. That had been done before, too. By Cane. It started when Snow was young, and Snow never liked it.

"If you are certain I took something," Snow said, "then explain to my lawyer why the U.S. government is so interested in getting it back." He knew the government cared more about protecting its secret than about sending him to jail.

"You don't seem to understand how much trouble you're in."

Snow shrugged.

"What do you want? A plea bargain?" Lemming asked.

Snow could feel Judge Stark's eyes on him.

Agent Lemming continued. "We are cooperating with 97 countries, each of which has evidence there was a break-in at the home of its head of state. What we have here is a pattern, one that ended when you stumbled at the White House and got caught."

Judge Stark said, "Are you going to keep me in suspense? What do you think my client stole?"

"It's top secret. A matter of national security."

Judge Stark laughed. "You can't prove my client stole something if you don't reveal what was stolen. You're making the U.S. attorney's job downright difficult, and mine a whole lot easier."

Agent Lemming sneered at Judge Stark. "We don't have to convict. We can classify this as an act of terrorism and hold your client for questioning for the next 20 years."

Snow saw a way to throw Lemming off his game. "The people above you haven't told you what's in the document I supposedly took from the White House, have they?"

"I don't have to answer questions. I take it you're not going to cooperate."

"Oh, I plan to cooperate," Snow said. "I plan to plead guilty."

Agent Lemming looked surprised. "And the document?"

Snow crossed his arms and leaned back in his chair. He could give up the document and save himself, but if he did, he'd sacrifice everything he'd worked to protect.

"Agent Lemming," Judge Stark said. "It appears that my client has nothing more to say to you at this time."

Monday, November 12th

Liz stood outside Tip Top Toy Company's plant and marveled at its size. She faced the front wall of the two-story building but she couldn't see the corners. "How big is it?" she asked Twirly.

"A square mile. Mighty big square mile, indeed!"

"You should see the inside," Henry added. "Goes on forever."

They were welcomed by a young girl who reminded Liz of Holly 11 years earlier.

"You must be Mistletoe," Liz said. "Elf-in-training, right?"

The elf beamed. "Yes, and my ears are getting pointier each day. Welcome to Tip Top Toy Company's headquarters where we make most of our toys."

Mistletoe led them on a tour of the toy manufacturing plant. It smelled like oiled machinery hard at work but seemed like familiar territory to Henry and Twirly. It opened Liz's eyes to a whole new piece of Santa's operation, an effective combination of elves and machines, each using the other to create an astounding output of toys.

"Over there," Mistletoe pointed, "is the children's toy section. Beyond it, down that side of the plant, you'll find clothes, electronics, games and musical instruments. The rest of the production modules, as well as packaging, storage and distribution are on the north and west sides of the plant."

During the tour, Liz was reminded of Twirly's house that the county tried to steal, where the elves did work on a smaller scale. Here, she saw more elves under one roof than she could have imagined, all hard at work, with cheer on their faces. It brightened her mood, despite the uncertainty that lay ahead.

"Is this where you made the Reindeer Hoverboard?"

"Not on this floor," Mistletoe said. "We have a production facility on the second floor for special projects. That's also where we have our corporate offices and the work room you will use. Follow me."

Mistletoe led them up the stairs to a room with "Santa Relocation Plan" painted on the door. It was a busy place, with 15 to 20 elves at work. Five or six were studying or making edits to construction drawings on the walls. Others were busy at computers or speaking on video lines with workers at the construction site. Mistletoe led Liz, Twirly and Henry over to a large model in the center of the room, a three-dimensional mock-up of the underground village. An elderly elf, smoking a pipe and dressed in blue overalls and a worn green ball cap, stood beside the model. He turned and smiled when they arrived.

"You must be Liz Raker," he said. "I'm Lucky, the superintendent of this project. It's nice to meet you."

Liz liked Lucky right away. He looked intelligent and had a calm demeanor, just right for the task at hand. "It's nice to meet you, too. I look forward to working with you." She suspected that Lucky got results based more on competence than luck, but she'd be glad to have a little luck on their side, too.

"I see you've brought some helpers with you." Lucky took the pipe from his mouth and used it to point at Twirly and Henry standing to Liz's left. "I suppose when it comes to saving Christmas, you can't be choosy, can you?" He smiled as he said it.

Twirly and Henry laughed. Liz thought these three must have an interesting past together and more than a few stories to tell.

Lucky took Liz aside and for the next 30 minutes he educated her on the progress of the construction and listened while Liz explained the additional work she wanted done.

"Good ideas," Lucky said. "We'll get right on it."

Before Lucky returned Liz to Mistletoe, he gave her the reports on the core samples. She would study them in more detail later.

Mistletoe collected Liz and showed her to a corner she could use to do her work. She set Liz up with a computer and office supplies.

Liz thought about what lay ahead. Her work was just one of several things that needed to go well to save Christmas, and there were lots of unanswered questions. "Do you have a room with video conference call capabilities?"

"Sure," Mistletoe said. "When do you need it?"

"The sooner the better," Liz said. It was time to get the Band of True Believers together.

After the Twirly Masters trial, Liz became concerned about what Hank Snow might do next, so she founded the Band of True Believers. Her dad showed her how to prepare bylaws. He, Sarah, Austin Land and Judge Stark all were BTB members. She liked to say, "We have two lawyers, a reporter, a judge and me to fight for Santa Claus in the real world."

While Mistletoe hustled off to secure the video-conference room, Liz explained what she was planning to Twirly and Henry, and sent text messages to the BTB members. She got quick responses. The call would take place within the hour.

Mistletoe returned to say everything was ready. "Mind me asking who you're calling?"

"A group known as the Band of True Believers," Liz said.

"I've heard of the BTB from my cousin, Holly."

"It's just something I started as a little girl. It's more about the people in it. I think they can help."

"Of course they can. We love adults who believe in Santa, but none have ever banded together to protect Santa except the BTB. You're an inspiration to all of Santa's elves."

"But we haven't done anything yet."

"You haven't had anything important to do—until now."

Through the magic of modern technology, Liz connected the BTB members via video teleconference. Liz called Raker and Sarah first. She could see their faces on the large monitor on the wall.

"Hey, Dad. Hey, Sarah!"

"Hey," they said together. Raker added, "What's this about? Is everything okay?"

"Yes and no. Wait a sec and I'll fill you in," Liz said. "We're going to have two more people join us."

"Who?" Sarah asked.

"The rest of the Band of True Believers."

"But Liz," Raker said, "that was just—"

"I know Dad, it was just something that a little girl thought up, but we need to work together if we want to save Christmas again."

Her next call was to Austin Land and Judge Stark, who were together because the judge had no idea how to video conference. "Hey, Austin. Hey, Judge Stark," Liz said. "Hello," they responded in unison.

Twirly, Henry and Mistletoe were in the room. Before she could continue, Twirly couldn't help himself. "Thad, it's great to see my lawyer again. Sarah, you look lovely, as usual. Looks like the two of you have another courtroom adventure on your hands. Yes, indeed. And Austin, hello to you. I've been reading your newspaper articles. Excellent reporting. Just splendid. And very nice to see you, Judge Stark. Last time I saw you was at my trial. Superb judging, yes, indeed."

Liz jumped in before Twirly could continue. She introduced Mistletoe and Henry said hello. Then she got down to business.

"I'd like to call this meeting of the Band of True Believers to order."

"Here, here," Judge Stark said. The others chimed in with support.

"You probably never thought the Band of True Believers would have a real job to do," Liz said. "Turns out, it does. Christmas is being threatened in our hometown and at the North Pole. The purpose of this call is to coordinate our efforts. I'd like Judge Stark to start off by sharing what he can about Hank Snow and then hear from everyone else."

"Thank you, Liz," Judge Stark said. "Last Wednesday, the FBI interviewed Hank Snow. The government is prepared to lock him up and throw away the key unless he turns over a document they say he took from the White House."

"Judge Stark," Sarah said, "why did Hank Snow break into the homes of presidents and prime ministers around the world, and why would he steal a document from the White House?"

"I'm sorry. I can't reveal what he told me. Attorney-client privilege."

"Even if it means saving Christmas?" Liz asked.

"I'm afraid so," Judge Stark said. "But I can tell you what the government learned through its forensic team and turned over in discovery. The day of the White House break-in, Snow sent an encrypted email attaching a copy of a document to Zachary Cane at the North Pole. Thirty seconds later, he forwarded the same email to a secure email address known as S-leaks@santa.com. In the second email, he said he was sending the original document to the recipient by regular mail."

"That address is a North Pole address," Twirly said, breaking in. "But I don't recognize the recipient, S-leaks."

"I can look into it," Mistletoe said.

"One more thing," Judge Stark said. "The email to S-leaks@santa.com said it was time to activate the SRP."

"I can explain that," Liz said. "It's called the Santa Relocation Plan, and it's why I'm in Greenland." She explained how the North Pole ice sheet was melting at an alarming rate, how Holly was hard at work on the secret project to move Santa and the elves to Greenland and how she was engaged in the assignment Tarina had given her to help ensure that the new underground village in Greenland was habitable.

"Judge Stark," Sarah said, "are the stolen document and the charges against Hank Snow connected to the environmental threat to the North Pole?"

"I can't tell you what Snow told me about that. The information is privileged."

"What about the hoverboard case?" Sarah asked.

"After Greenback served Snow with his subpoena to testify, I asked Snow about Tarina Winter and Tip Top Toy Company, but he changed the subject. My hunch is that Snow is working on a plan and he's just waiting until the right time to clue me in."

"Judge Stark," Liz asked, "do you think Hank Snow will cooperate in the hoverboard lawsuit? If Tip Top Toy Company loses the case, Tarina won't be able to provide the land for Santa's new village."

"I can't be sure."

"Does he still plan to plead guilty to the criminal charges?" Sarah asked.

"He does. He refuses to tell me why, but I suspect it has to do with his unwillingness to acknowledge what he truly does for a living."

"Sounds like the Hank Snow I remember," Raker said.

Liz wondered why her dad had been so quiet. She knew he didn't trust Hank Snow and probably thought Snow was getting what he deserved by being in jail.

"I've arranged to delay the date for Snow to enter his plea until December 24th," Judge Stark said, "with the hope that we can sort things out before then."

"That's good," Liz said. "In the meantime, we should focus on Zachary Cane, chairman of the Elf High Council. He arrested Holly for telling the truth about global warming and he's done nothing to address the fact that the ice sheet at the North Pole is going to collapse. Holly is not sure Santa's village will stand up until Christmas."

"Wait," Henry said. "Cane isn't chairman. Hank Snow is."

"Cane declared Snow missing in action and took over," Liz said.

"I know where he is," Judge Stark said, "as do the media, and the news is all over the Internet. You would think Cane would know."

Mistletoe jumped into the conversation. "Before I was stationed at Tip Top Toy Company, I was a clerk for the Elf High Council. Ran errands. Made copies. My ears weren't very pointy but I could hear just the same. I think Mr. Cane is jealous of Hank Snow. I'm sure he knows where Hank Snow is, and he wants him to stay there."

"I agree," Twirly said. "Henry and I have known Cane for a long time. He and Hank Snow have a complicated relationship."

"True," Henry said. "Zachary Cane is the oldest elf in Santa's village. He was an elf of authority long before Hank Snow had any power. Over the years, Hank Snow rose through the ranks, and he paid his dues, serving in every department and working in every position. Cane told the community that he was grooming Hank Snow to be his successor, and said he was glad the elves voted Snow to be chairman this year. Said he was glad to be the vice chairman, but I've noticed a few things. It may be jealousy, but it could be more than that."

"What do you mean?" Liz asked.

"Cane is a disciplinarian. Hard on the workers. Unbending. Secretive. No heart for the children."

"Sounds a little bit like Hank Snow," Raker said.

"True," Henry said. "Snow has emulated Cane in many ways, but if he hadn't, he never would have risen to be chairman of the Elf High Council. At the time of my trial, I thought Snow was responsible for modifying the algorithm for the Naughty and Nice lists, but I learned later that the decision to be stricter when classifying children as Nice was Cane's. Snow simply developed the technology to make it happen."

"Interesting," Twirly said. "Interesting, indeed. Remember how Snow conspired with the county to take my land, which would have closed an important distribution center for Santa? I learned later that Cane had ordered Snow to give away my land and lay off my elves to slash costs. Snow was trying to do something creative with drone technology to keep deliveries going in the area. We know how that failed."

"I've always wondered about Snow's motives," Raker said. "I never understood why he fought against us in those two trials."

"Maybe there was more to it," Henry said. "Cover-ups have always been Cane's specialty. He always insisted on it. Maybe Snow knew that and figured he had to play along to win Cane's confidence."

Liz looked at Sarah and her dad. "How's the hoverboard lawsuit coming?"

"The information I'm getting in depositions is helpful, but the judge is being difficult," Sarah said.

"It's true," Raker said. "Judge Johnson is determined to retaliate against me for winning Twirly's case 11 years ago. It embarrassed him. He may rule that Santa is fake, throw out our defense and enter judgment for the plaintiffs."

"But if that happens," Twirly said, "Tip Top Toy Company goes out of business and loses the land for Santa's new home. Yes, indeed."

There was an uneasy ebb in the conversation in response to Twirly's words. "I wonder if we can pull this off." Liz said.

"Never give up hope, Liz," Henry said.

"He's right, Liz," Raker said. "All we can do is our best."

"Well said," Judge Stark added. "Always believe!"

"That's it," Austin Land said. "We need more believers."

"Interesting thought," Judge Stark said. "What do you have in mind?"

"How about a social media campaign to get some public sympathy for Tip Top Toy Company and the Santa Relocation Plan? Judge, I know you didn't care too much for my tweets and newspaper articles during Henry's trial but you have to admit, they worked."

"You're right," Judge Stark said. "You turned public opinion to Henry's side. It might do the same for Tip Top Toy Company. You can keep the pressure on the nonbelievers and pick up new believers in the process. Maybe it will help Hank Snow, too."

"Let's not forget," Raker said, "saving Christmas and saving Hank Snow are not the same thing."

Judge Stark laughed. "I don't know, Thad. Whenever and wherever Hank Snow shows up in your life, Christmas gets saved. He may be the link to our success."

Tuesday, November 27th

In the two weeks following the BTB conference call, Austin Land created a robust and diverse social media platform to advance the goals of the Band of True Believers. He built a dynamic web page devoted to informing the world that Santa's village was at imminent risk of collapse due to global warming, and he registered the domain name, you-better-watch-out.com. He linked it to another website under the domain name, you-better-not-pout.com. The first website focused on a post-apocalyptic world devoid of Santa's North Pole, and the second urged believers to pay attention to the ecologic forces at work before it's too late.

The social media platform included a "Santa on Thin Ice" Facebook page. Land posted images on it of what was left of the North Pole's current ice sheet, the foundation for Santa's village. He drove traffic to the site with ads that warned naughtiness would rule the land if the North Pole village collapsed.

Land's strategy included a LinkedIn account for Santa. It had a picture of the jolly elf, along with a history of his career in the toy distribution business. On the landing page, it said: "Please congratulate Santa on his retirement." It linked to an article that explained how the environment had forced Santa to retire early.

Land also created an eBay account to dispose of Santa's belongings at bargain prices. The message: Santa won't need any of the items when the North Pole ice sheet vanishes. One ad said: "Toy-making tools at half-cost." Another ad said: "One red suit, worn only once a year, available at one-third cost." A third ad offered the best deal: "Reindeer available free as pets. Well-trained."

Land published a blog post called: "How the Carbon Emission Stole Christmas." Next, he edited a piece for the New York Times called: "Is Global Warming the End for the North Pole?" He then finalized an article slated for publication in 75 college student newspapers that Liz helped write, titled: "The Connection Between Global Warming and Rising Interest Rates on Student Loans." Similar articles were scheduled to show up in publications across the world in December. The message: Global warming is real. A threat not just to sea levels around the world, but to the North Pole. To Santa Claus. To the public. And to Christmas, itself.

It didn't take long to see results. Students at colleges all over the world had sit-ins and government offices were swamped with letters, emails and phone calls from people who wanted to save Christmas. Santa trended on Facebook, Instagram and Twitter.

But there was pushback, too. The League of Informed Entrepreneurs labeled the work fake news and published its own version of the truth. Land stayed busy pointing out that their version was the fake news. He chastised LIE's role in the Tip Top Toy Company case with tweets that used hashtags, including #TheLeagueofSantaHaters and #TheReindeerHoverBoardDoesFly.

Land knew that the public reaction generated by LIE's opposition to Tip Top Toy Company and the Santa Relocation Plan would be more helpful than harmful. It would bring the talking heads into play. Cable networks would start putting resources into covering the story and once the Santa connection took hold, the hoverboard lawsuit and the melting ice sheet would be the top worldwide story. Land hoped it would be in time to make a difference.

Thursday, December 6th

Zachary Cane called an unofficial meeting of the Elf High Council. It was unofficial because Cane invited only two of the other three members. He saw no need to include Snowflake. She might be in charge of The Archives, but she wasn't in charge of running the North Pole. He was, and he needed to cement the Council's opposition to Hank Snow.

For years, Cane trusted Snow, because Snow did everything asked of him. He worked in every department as Cane's spy, and he took Cane's side when Cane banished Tarina Winter. The woman had been a thorn in Cane's side, always demanding rights for the workers and seeking a more democratic form of government. The North Pole was not a democracy, and Winter was never seen or heard from again.

The Tarina Winter solution cemented Cane's trust in Snow and Cane offered to promote Snow to second in command, but Snow requested to be head of security, a position he held for 130 years, until just after the Henry Edmonds trial. Cane was impressed with how Snow handled himself in that trial and promoted Snow to chief operating officer. Snow held that position until after the Twirly Masters trial. It was Cane's idea to shut down Masters' distribution center and Snow took the blame when the plan failed. At that point, Cane nominated him for a vacant seat on the Elf High Council and ensured that the elves elected him.

Cane thought he could count on Snow. That was why he suggested that Snow take his place as chairman. That way, Cane avoided the work but knew that Snow would do his bidding. Gradually, though, he'd come to suspect that Snow was too much like himself. Deceptive and manipulative. It was time to throw Snow under the sleigh.

"I called you together to share some terrible information I've received about former Chairman Hank Snow."

The two elves perked up.

"Hank Snow has—"

The door opened and Snowflake walked in. "Hello, sirs. I'm sorry I'm late."

Cane was not happy to see Snowflake. She must have sources he didn't know about and he didn't trust her, but he continued without comment. Even if she didn't buy what he was saying, he had to sell it to the other two elves. "I was about to say when you walked in that we've received some bad news about Hank Snow."

"I know," Snowflake said, "he's in jail in the United States. We have to help him."

"That's not the bad news and no, we don't have to help him."

"What do you mean?" one of the old elves asked.

Cane had thought about what he was going to say. Just before Snow was arrested, Snow had emailed Cane with a recommendation, but Cane didn't like what Snow suggested. He thought Snow would remain loyal but he hadn't. It was best that Snow remain in jail.

"As you know," Cane said, "Hank Snow was supposed to assess the security risks to Santa of delivering presents to the official residences of the heads of state of approximately 100 countries.

But he violated orders and stole confidential information."

"What did he steal?" the other old elf asked.

"Mineral reports. Many countries are interested in what's below the surface at the North Pole. They want to push us out and claim the prize beneath our feet."

"It sounds to me," Snowflake said, "as if Mr. Snow wanted to protect us."

"I thought so, too," Cane said, "until I read his email. He suggested we persuade the village to evacuate because of global warming so that he and I could take the spoils for ourselves."

"That's treason," one of the old elves said.

"Calls for banishment," the other old elf said.

"May I see the email?" Snowflake asked.

"Unfortunately, no," Cane said. "He embedded a code that deleted the email once it was read. He was trying to cover his tracks in case I didn't go along with his plan."

"Very convenient," Snowflake said.

Cane didn't like her questioning tone.

"What do you suggest we do?" one of the old elves asked.

"We don't help him," Cane said. "We let him face the consequences in the U.S. for felony breaking and entering and we issue an edict prohibiting any resident of the North Pole from providing aid or support to him. If he is convicted, then we banish him from the North Pole."

"Excuse me, Mr. Cane," Snowflake said. "If he is convicted for felony breaking and entering, it's because he was caught trying to protect the North Pole, Christmas and Santa. I cannot vote to banish him for that."

"Then banish him for trying to deceive the village and steal the minerals."

"But I don't have any evidence that is what he tried to do."

Cane saw the two old elves look with surprise at Snowflake, and knew he had them in his corner.

"Let's take a vote," Cane said.

The vote was 3-to-1. "Good," Cane said. "We will print an edict prohibiting any assistance to Snow in his trial. Once Snow is convicted in the U.S., we will banish him from the North Pole, without the need of a hearing."

The two old elves bowed and began to leave.

"Before you go," Cane said, "there is one more thing. It's about Holly's trial."

"Do you think it proper, sir," Snowflake asked, "to discuss her trial before the evidence is presented?"

"Yes. Absolutely. The preservation of the North Pole depends upon avoiding panic. Holly and her friend, Liz Raker, will try to convince the elves that global warming is real, and we should leave the North Pole. We need to stand firm against that message."

"Why?" Snowflake asked. "Don't we need to listen to the evidence with open minds?"

He ignored her and spoke to the other elves. "Snow's lawyer and Liz Raker are close allies. The lawyer may try to bargain Snow's way out of jail by offering North Pole minerals to the U.S. government, with the assurance that the villagers will vacate the ice sheet. If we leave, we give the U.S. government the key to the village and reward Snow's treason. When you hear Holly and Liz Raker talk about the need to leave our home, you better think about Hank Snow."

Everyone was quiet.

"There you go," Cane said. "If Holly wins and we vacate the North Pole, Santa won't have a home. And for what? An environmental lie to free Hank Snow?"

"You want us to vote to banish Holly and declare global warming to be a hoax?" Snowflake asked.

"That's the size of it," Cane said. The other two elves nodded in support.

Wednesday, December 12th

Liz was hard at work at Tip Top Toy Company headquarters when her phone rang. It was Holly.

"How's the work on the underground village coming?" Holly asked.

"We're making great progress," Liz said. "Final inspection is scheduled for the 18th and then I catch the boat to come to you for your trial. How's the mood at the North Pole?"

"The elves are concerned. Most of them know there is a problem, and those who won't admit it are still worried we may be right. Cane, of course, continues to be adamant that there's nothing to be worried about. He's used the morning and afternoon editions of the Daily Candy Cane to run articles full of propaganda."

Liz saw Lucky come into the room, followed by several elves. Lucky was smoking his pipe as he gave directions to the elves. It looked like he had things well in hand and it helped ease the tension Liz felt while listening to Holly talk about Cane.

"What's the latest ecological activity on the ice sheet?" Liz asked.

"Not good," Holly said. "The ice pack makes a groaning noise every night like it's hurting. I don't have a good feeling about the village lasting until Christmas."

"How does Snowflake feel about it?"

"Optimistic as ever. You know Snowflake. She says she believes in Hank Snow, in me, in you, in your dad, in Sarah and in Tarina."

Liz had been so busy with her work that she hadn't had a chance to ask Holly about Hank Snow's past and his relationship with Zachary Cane. On the call with the BTB, it sounded like Cane, not Snow, might be the one to blame for interfering in the trials of Henry Edmonds and Twirly Masters, but it was Snow who was in jail for felony breaking and entering. "Do you think Hank Snow was doing something illegal for Cane at the White House? Do you think Snow can be trusted?"

"Snowflake trusts him and I've been asking around," Holly said. "Many of the elves do not like Zachary Cane but every time I mentioned Hank Snow, their eyes lit up. Like Snowflake, they didn't explain themselves, but one of the oldest female elves in the village referred to Hank Snow as 'the one.' She's the midwife who delivered him."

"I don't understand," Liz said. "What does she mean by 'the one?'"

"She said Snow was born from greatness."

"Who are his parents?"

"That's what I found most interesting. He was born in Greenland, but that's all she would say. She wouldn't tell me the names of his parents."

"What does Snowflake think?"

"Snowflake knows the truth but she's not telling me. I found a clue in an old book at The Archives, but Snowflake said it's not her story to tell."

"What did you find?"

"A family tree. Santa and Mrs. Claus had a child but the record was deleted, perhaps for the protection of the child and family."

"Protection from whom?" Liz asked.

"I'm guessing Zachary Cane," Holly said.

Liz thought about what Holly said, but couldn't come to terms with what her mind suggested. "Holly, this sounds crazy, but do you think Hank Snow is Santa's son?"

"I've wondered the same thing," Holly said. "When I confronted Snowflake with the suggestion last week, she didn't admit or deny it."

"If it's true," Liz said, "the future of Christmas could be going to prison for a long, long time."

"But he has a good lawyer," Holly said.

"You're right about that. Judge Stark will do all he can to save Christmas, and if saving Christmas means saving Hank Snow, he'll work even harder."

Tuesday, December 18th

The courtroom bustled with people when Raker and Tarina arrived. With 15 minutes until the hearing started, there were only a few spectator seats left.

"Who are all these people?" Raker asked the clerk, who met him in the aisle.

"Supporters of the League of Informed Entrepreneurs."

"Look like a bunch of nonbelieving idiots to me," Tarina said.

"Remember," Raker said, "you need to keep calm."

He guided her to their table and unloaded his briefcase. When he looked up, he saw Greenback and Brighthouse deep in conversation. He wondered what they were planning. Probably the end of Christmas.

The side door opened, the bailiff announced the Honorable Cleve R. Johnson's presence and the judge took his seat.

"Honorable," Tarina muttered. "We'll see about that."

Raker sighed.

Sarah Kennedy slipped in behind Raker, deposited a banker's box full of files under the table and took her place between her husband and their client.

Johnson looked around the courtroom. "Why the crowd, Mr. Greenback?"

"Just supporters, your honor."

"Make sure they behave."

The courtroom door swung open and Judge Johnson looked past Greenback toward the person who entered. "You're late, Mr. Stark. Maybe I should confiscate your watch like you did mine in the Twirly Masters trial." Raker turned to see Judge Stark coming up the aisle.

"Don't bother. I don't wear a watch." Judge Stark winked at Raker.

"No excuse for being late."

"I'm not late. My client is not a party to this proceeding. Just a witness. I thought I'd come early and watch the show." Judge Stark pointed at the wall above Judge Johnson's head. "The portrait behind you looks a touch better. Duct tape is a wonderful thing."

Johnson looked over his shoulder in disgust at the damaged portrait and turned his attention back to Greenback. "How many witnesses do you have for this hearing?"

"Your honor, we have a thousand witnesses who—"

"You have what?" Johnson was apoplectic.

"Don't worry, your honor. These witnesses have signed affidavits. We don't plan to call them to testify live. They represent a sample of the 100,000 class members. You will find their stories to be entirely consistent. May I approach?"

Greenback took two binders up and handed them to Judge Johnson.

"Summarize these for me, Mr. Greenback."

"Each affiant saw an online advertisement for the Reindeer Hoverboard. Bought it. Unwrapped it. Stepped on it. Nothing happened. Nothing. It didn't move. It certainly didn't fly as advertised."

132

"That's all?"

"No, your honor. We had each purchaser say whether they read the warning label. They did."

"And?"

"They had no idea what a True Believer was. Figured it was someone who believed the hoverboard would fly. They were hoodwinked."

"Any other witnesses?"

"Yes, your honor. We plan to call Mr. Stubble, the class representative, and Dr. A. J. Wright, the doctor who performed Ms. Winter's psychiatric examination. In rebuttal to defendant's witnesses, we will call Hank Snow. He'll be the last witness you hear from."

"What about you, Ms. Brighthouse? Any witnesses?"

"Yes, your honor. Paul Wingnut, Ph.D., founder of LIE. He led the study on the harms caused to children and businesses by the Santa lie."

"Raker?"

"Tarina Winter will be our only live witness. We also have affidavits and deposition testimony for the court to consider."

"Affidavits and depositions from whom?"

"I'll let Ms. Kennedy answer that question."

"How many affidavits, Ms. Kennedy?"

"Fifty."

"That's it? Mr. Greenback has a thousand."

"It's not the quantity of the evidence that matters, your honor, but the quality of the evidence."

"True," Judge Johnson said, "but I'm the one who determines what's quality and what's not. Who signed these 50 affidavits?"

"True Believers."

Someone from the audience heckled: "She lies."

Judge Johnson grabbed his new gavel and slammed it on the bench. "No comments from the audience." He pointed the gavel at Sarah. "What are you trying to do here?"

"Put on our case." Sarah was serious and professional. Raker wasn't sure he would be so calm.

"And what do these so-called True Believers say, exactly?"

"They bought Reindeer Hoverboards from my client. They believe in Santa Claus. Their hoverboards worked. Simple as that."

Greenback got to his feet. "We object to these affidavits, Judge Johnson."

"Go on." Judge Johnson seemed interested in a way to sustain the objection.

"This is a pathetic attempt to get in front of a jury. They have 50 deluded adults saying they believe in Santa Claus to throw a cog in the wheels of justice. We move the affidavits be stricken because the signers are incompetent."

"He's got a point, Ms. Kennedy. Why should I accept affidavits from adults who say that Santa Claus is real?"

"Competence is a not the issue, your honor."

"Are you saying that if you brought me 50 affidavits from people who say the world is flat, I have to force the taxpayers to fund a jury trial to decide that question?"

"No," Sarah said, "The issue is whether the hoverboard is defective, and these affidavits show that the hoverboard worked for witnesses who believe in Santa Claus. If you strike the affidavits, you exclude material evidence."

"Your honor," Greenback's voice boomed, "material means legally relevant. There is nothing material to this lawsuit about the existence of Santa Claus. It's a farcical grasping at straws. Not a legal defense recognized by sound jurisprudence."

"What do you have to say to that, Ms. Kennedy?"

"We have 25 deposition transcripts from the class of plaintiffs that support our argument."

"Summarize them," Judge Johnson said.

"They all admit a very important fact."

"What's that?"

"The Reindeer Hoverboard didn't work for them but it worked for all their children who ranged in ages from 5 to 9."

"To use Mr. Greenback's term, how is that material?"

Sarah smiled. "I thought that would be self-evident, your honor. All these children believe in Santa Claus. Their parents don't. The hoverboards worked for the children but not their parents. The explanation for why the hoverboard didn't fly for their parents is obvious."

Tammy Brighthouse was on her feet. "We object, your honor. LIE's mission is to protect children from false tales about a jolly old elf who flies around the world in a sleigh. There could be any number of reasons why the hoverboards worked for the children and not the adults. Weight distribution. Balance. Coordination. Battery life."

"Ms. Kennedy," Judge Johnson said, "for you to advance your argument, you need the testimony of the children. Your husband says you only plan to call Ms. Winter as a witness."

Tarina Winter spoke up, from her seated position. "That was my decision, judge."

Raker looked at his client and got the feeling that she was intent on picking a fight with the man who was going to decide her company's fate.

"And why did you make that decision?" Judge Johnson had his gavel at the ready.

"Because children deserve the right to be free of closed-minded adults like you and the collection of fools that surround us in this courtroom." Her arm swung in a wide arc around the room as she made her point. It was as if she wanted to get locked up.

There were shouts from the audience. "Liar. Liar!"

Bang. The gavel came down. Bang. Bang. Bang. Raker thought it was about to slip from Judge Johnson's hand again and damage something else in the room.

"Ms. Winter, I am holding you in contempt of court. You will spend the next 24 hours in the county jail. Bailiff, take her into custody."

Raker and Kennedy objected but it did no good. They would have to defend Tip Top Toy Company on the first day of the hearing without its owner to help them.

As the bailiff escorted Tarina from the room, the audience hooted, but she held her head high. She looked elegant, handling the calamity with style. Not a hint of fear. You'd have thought the bailiff was a headwaiter showing her to her favorite table.

At the door, with her wrists locked behind her back, she turned to face her lawyers and mouthed two words: "Always believe." Then she winked at them.

Same Day – 10:00 a.m.

"Call your first witness, Mr. Greenback." Judge Johnson was ready to move this hearing along. No dallying.

"We call Dr. A. J. Wright."

Good, Johnson thought. He wanted to hear this. He waved the doctor to the witness stand and she swore to tell the truth. The woman seemed annoyed to be there. Perhaps she would talk fast.

Greenback asked questions about her education, degrees, specialties, experience, honors, awards, papers and grants. He then asked about her experience as an expert witness. "Dr. Wright, have you ever examined patients to determine their fitness to testify in court?"

"Hundreds of times," she said.

"And have you ever appeared in court as an expert witness?"

"Yes."

"About the fitness of a person to testify?"

"Yes."

"Often?"

"At least 50 times."

"Your honor," Greenback said, "I offer Dr. Wright as an expert witness in personality and psychiatric disorders."

How could Johnson refuse? The woman was overqualified for the task at hand. Heck, he didn't have a medical degree and he was qualified to say that an adult who believes in Santa Claus is crazy. If he could do it, she could, too. "Yes, she can testify as an expert," Judge Johnson said.

Greenback beamed at his witness. "Did you conduct a psychiatric examination of Tarina Winter, the president of Tip Top Toy Company?"

"I did."

"Was the patient cooperative?"

"Combative would be a better description."

Judge Johnson could relate to that. He found himself nodding in agreement.

"Did you gather enough information to render an opinion?" Greenback asked.

"Yes."

"What is your opinion, based on your extensive medical training and experience, as to the mental capacity of Tarina Winter?"

"The woman knows right from wrong, but she has a delusion."

Judge Johnson sat up. He had read the doctor's report, but he wanted to hear an expert say in open court that Tarina Winter was incompetent.

"Does it have to do with Santa Claus?"

"Not Santa, per se, but someone close to him."

"Please explain."

"Ms. Winter believes she is the daughter of Mrs. Claus."

Members of the audience started laughing. "Tell it, Doc," someone shouted.

Johnson banged his gavel to regain order, but his swing didn't pack much of a punch. He was enjoying the testimony.

When the laughter died down, Greenback continued. "Is she competent to testify?"

"Not in my opinion."

"That's all we have for this witness, your honor."

"You're up, Mr. Raker."

"Thank you, your honor."

Even though Raker observed the niceties, Judge Johnson saw he had a look about him. He was going to try to make the witness look bad.

Raker picked up a document. "Dr. Wright, you prepared a medical report on your examination of Tarina Winter, correct?"

"I did."

"And in that report, you called Ms. Winter paranoid, delusional, irrational, combative and uncooperative."

"Yes, sir. She was a difficult patient with serious personality disorders."

"And were all of those personality disorders, as you call them, related to this one fact she gave you?"

"I wouldn't call her relationship to Mrs. Claus a fact."

Johnson liked this doctor. He hoped Raker would ask a few more foolish questions.

"Fair enough, Dr. Wright. I take it you don't believe in Santa Claus?"

"No, sir."

"As a child, did you believe in Santa Claus?"

"I did, but that was—"

"When you were a child, were you ever diagnosed as being paranoid, delusional or irrational, because of your belief in Santa Claus?"

"Mr. Raker, I—"

"Just answer the question, please."

"No, I was not so diagnosed."

Raker changed the subject. "What do you know about Tarina Winter?"

"I know she thinks her mother is Mrs. Claus."

"And that's the reason you find her to be incompetent?"

"Yes."

"Do you know her mother?"

"Are you joking, Mr. Raker?"

"No, I'm asking if you know her mother. Better yet, do you know what her mother's full name is, or where her mother lives?"

"That was not part of—"

"Not part of your assessment. Why not? You're diagnosing Tarina Winter as being incompetent to testify because she says her mother is Mrs. Claus. Are you saying there is no mother in this world with the last name Claus?"

"She was talking about Santa's wife."

"I'm sorry, I thought you said Santa Claus is not real. How could he have a wife?"

Judge Johnson glared at Raker. Greenback needed to do something.

"Objection," Greenback said, "badgering the witness."

"Sustained." He hoped Greenback would be on his toes.

"Your honor" Raker said, "The doctor brought up Mrs. Claus. The rules of evidence permit me to cross-examine her on the subject. I ask that you reconsider your ruling. Otherwise, the court is hearing only half the story."

The judge thought about the request and decided he would let Raker cross-examine the doctor so that he would have no ground for appeal. He could declare Tarina Winter incompetent anyway, so it didn't matter. "Mr. Raker, I take your point. You may proceed."

"Dr. Wright, did Tarina Winter say her father was Santa Claus?"

"I don't recall."

"Do you need to see your report to refresh your recollection?"

"I have a copy." Dr. Wright reached into her satchel and pulled out the report. Raker asked her to turn to Page 3.

"What did she say about Santa Claus?"

She scanned the page and found the answer. "She said she never wanted Santa to be her father."

"So, she never said that Santa was her father, did she?"

Dr. Wright read the rest of the page. "Give me just a minute, please."

"Take your time," Raker said.

The doctor flipped through all the pages. Johnson hoped she would find the answer she needed. After a few minutes, she looked resigned.

"No, Mr. Raker, she never said her father was Santa Claus."

Raker's cadence picked up. "Is it possible, Dr. Wright, that you misunderstood what Tarina Winter told you? Is it possible that she does have a mother with the last name Claus, who has nothing to do with Santa Claus?"

Greenback objected. "Your honor, it sounds like Mr. Raker is undermining his client's defense."

"He's got a point, Mr. Raker," Judge Johnson said. "How do you square your client's defense with your cross-examination?"

"I don't have to, your honor. This witness, Dr. Wright, is telling this court that Tarina Winter is delusional. That's all I'm focused on at the moment, whether her expert opinion is sound. I intend to show that Dr. Wright is not right, after all."

The judge clinched his jaw. Raker was making this more difficult that it needed to be. "Proceed."

"Dr. Wright," Raker said, "I asked you a question. Is it possible that Ms. Winter has a mother with the last name Claus?"

"I suppose it's possible."

"And if she does, would that fact—that fact alone—make her crazy? Incompetent to testify?"

Dr. Wright looked trapped. She looked to Greenback, who didn't appear to have any help to offer. She placed the report back in her satchel, straightened her dress and said, "No, sir, that fact does not make her incompetent."

"That's all I have for this witness," Raker said.

Johnson wasn't pleased. He didn't have enough to find Tarina Winter incompetent. He called a short recess.

Same Day – 10:30 a.m.

The bailiff guided Tarina Winter into the processing center of the county jail. He stepped forward and handed Judge Johnson's written order to the magistrate, who was seated behind a small desk. While the magistrate read the order, the bailiff pushed her up to the front of the desk.

The magistrate looked at Tarina. "Contempt, huh? You don't look like the kind who creates a scene in court."

Tarina didn't respond. The magistrate shrugged, stamped the order "received" and noted the date and time on the document. She handed keys to the

147

bailiff and said, "Put her in the holding cell next to the other witness Judge Johnson wants in court tomorrow."

The bailiff guided Tarina down a narrow hallway to the oldest part of the jail. He unlocked a door to a poorly lit room with two side-by-side cells. Each cell had steel bars from floor to ceiling. Only one cell was occupied. By the man Tarina had come to see.

"Turn around," the bailiff said. She did and he unfastened her handcuffs. She felt Hank Snow watch her as the bailiff nudged her into her cell. He backed out, slammed the door, turned the key in the lock and attached the key to his belt. Tarina grabbed a bar with each hand and leaned forward. "Thank you, sir. You've been most helpful."

"Judge is right. You are crazy," the bailiff said. He walked through the main door, but before he pulled it shut, he said, "Enjoy your stay."

The echo of the closing door faded and left the room quiet.

Clap. Pause. Clap. Pause. Clap. Clap. Clap. "Well done," Snow said.

Tarina looked into the cell next to hers to see the former chairman of the Elf High Council lying on his back on a cot, looking at the ceiling above him.

"You could have just asked to see me," he said.

"You would have said no."

"You're right. I would have." He didn't look at her.

Tarina moved to the cot in her cell and sat. She knew she had to be patient. Hank Snow would have questions. He'd been locked up for too long. Two hours passed before Snow asked the first question. "Does Raker know?"

"Know what? You and I have a lot of secrets."

"Does he know about our past?"

"Let's see. He doesn't know you're my brother. Nor does he know that our mother is married to Santa Claus. Nor does he know that our companies do business together."

"Good," Snow said.

"Oh, and if it makes any difference, he doesn't know that you conspired with Zachary Cane to banish me from the North Pole 150 years ago."

Snow got up and moved to the far corner of his cell, with his back to the wall. An elf in the shadows. Just like he'd always been to her.

"It couldn't be helped," he said.

"Everything can be helped when it comes to family. You sided with Zachary Cane instead of your sister."

"Times were difficult."

This brought Tarina to her feet. She walked across her cell to the bars that kept her from slapping her brother. The 10 feet that separated them was as close as they'd been in 150 years. She'd done business with Snow and North Pole Enterprises over the years at the request of her mother to help Santa, but she'd always spoken with Snow by phone and it was always about business. Being with him in person opened this old wound.

"I trusted you," she said. "You let me down."

"Is that how you see it?"

"How else could I possibly see it?"

"What? You don't like Greenland?"

"It's a beautiful place to live," Tarina said, "but you wouldn't know because you never bothered to visit."

"I don't know why you're complaining," he said. "You never had to leave Santa's business and, as you said, you live in a beautiful place."

Tarina was surprised. She didn't think Snow knew the secret of Tip Top Toy Company's connection to Santa's North Pole operations. "How do you know I didn't leave Santa's business?"

"You mean how do I know that you and Mom founded Tip Top Toy Company? Or maybe you're asking me how I know that Tip Top Toy Company meets half the North Pole's distribution requirements, employs half the world's elf community and is working to provide a safe haven for Santa's village before it collapses?"

"So you do know. You should be thanking me," Tarina said. It was obvious her brother didn't appreciate her help. It made her angry. "I suppose your next move is to side with the hoverboard plaintiffs to get me out of the way once and for all."

"No, I don't want you to lose. We need to relocate the village to Greenland."

"How about that," Tarina said, "Hank Snow has a heart. Or are you just worried you will lose your power if your subordinates disappear into the sea?"

"No. I expect I will be in prison."

Tarina was stumped. This was not like her brother. He was putting other people before himself, and it gave her a thought. Maybe he would open up if she shared what she knew. It was worth a try.

"Cane has resumed the chairmanship in your absence," Tarina said, "and told the Elf High Council that you committed treason. The elves are barred from helping you and if you're convicted here in the U.S., you will be banished from the North Pole."

"I'm not surprised. I suspected that Cane is the one who betrayed me. What has he said I've done?"

"Something about you finding a document concerning minerals at the North Pole. He said you sent him the document and proposed that he and you keep the minerals for yourselves."

"I did find the document and I did send it to him, but he's twisted the facts. My mission was and continues to be to help the North Pole."

Tarina wasn't sure she could trust her brother, but she'd much rather have him run Santa's operations than Zachary Cane. "Look, Cane is our common enemy. He wants you to rot in jail and he wants to kill the Santa Relocation Plan. I'm sure he wants Tip Top Toy Company to lose this case. For goodness sake, you and I have the same blood in our veins and our mother is the most powerful First Lady in the world. If we work together, Cane can't stop us."

"He doesn't know about you or Tip Top Toy Company," Snow said. "I've kept that secret."

"That gives us an edge." Tarina wasn't sure what to make of this good deed by her brother.

Snow chuckled. "I should have gotten out of the way and let you take on Cane years ago. You'd have kicked him to the curb and taken over."

"Better yet," Tarina said, "let's kick him to the edge of the ice sheet and ask him whether he wants to swim or come to his senses."

"Tarina, if the plaintiffs think we're working together they won't call me as a witness. If I don't testify, you lose, so you need to continue to be antagonistic and unforgiving toward me. Same goes for your lawyers. Don't tip them off."

"Tip them off as to what?" Tarina asked. "I have no idea what you're up to."

"Good," Snow said. "Let's keep it that way."

Tarina didn't like it, but her brother had a plan and she didn't, so she decided to go along with it for now, even though it left her in the dark.

"Why doesn't Cane believe Santa's village is sinking?" she asked.

"He doesn't want to believe it. He's blinded himself to the truth."

"But the future of Christmas is at stake," she said.

"You don't know Cane's history, do you?" Snow asked.

"I never cared to find out," Tarina said "I always saw him as a selfish bureaucrat who didn't take care of the elves who worked for Santa."

"That's pretty close," Snow said. He explained that Cane was expelled for high treason from an elf clan that lived in the Norwegian archipelago of Svalbard, and wound up living alone at the North

Pole. Santa was unaware of Cane's past when he approached Cane about using the remote location to establish his village. Cane made a deal with him.

"Let me guess. There was a catch."

"You got it. They set up a form of government where the Elf High Council, which was controlled by Cane, has most of the power. Santa took on the limited-government role of a modern-day monarch, a position with mostly ceremonial duties, like the right to confer honors—presents, for example—but no governing authority."

"Do you think Cane cares if Christmas survives?" Tarina asked.

"He's never cared about Christmas. Only his power and his property."

"But—"

"Tarina, you have to understand something about Cane. He's like the stubborn captain of a leaking ship, prepared to go down with his vessel to protect his gold cargo and take all his passengers with him."

The situation was worse than Tarina suspected. "If what you say is true, we have little chance of saving Christmas with Cane in control."

Same Day – 11:00 a.m.

"Call your next witness, Mr. Greenback." Johnson hoped Greenback would do a better job with this witness.

"We call Martin Stubble, the class representative."

"Come around and be sworn, Mr. Stubble." Judge Johnson noticed that Sarah Kennedy had taken the defense counsel seat closest to the witness box. That meant she would probably do the cross-examination.

After the introduction and pleasantries, Greenback asked about the Reindeer Hoverboard. "Did it work?"

"Not at all."

Greenback turned behind him and picked up a brand new Reindeer Hoverboard. "May I approach the witness, your honor?"

When permission was granted, he walked between his table and the table where Sarah and Raker were sitting. As he tried to carry the toy through the small space, the back end of the hoverboard bumped Sarah on the shoulder.

"Excuse me, "Greenback said.

But that wasn't what drew Judge Johnson's attention. When the hoverboard touched Sarah on the shoulder, LED lights down its sides began to flicker and the board made a humming sound like a car idling. Then it stopped.

"What was that?" Judge Johnson asked.

"It does that sometimes, judge," Stubble said. "It has some kind of short in it."

Greenback kept walking until he stood in front of the witness box. "Mr. Stubble, is this the Reindeer Hoverboard you purchased from Tip Top Toy Company?"

"That's it."

"Your honor, we'd like to mark this as Exhibit 1 and enter it into evidence."

"Admitted."

The clerk put an exhibit sticker on the hoverboard, and Greenback leaned it against the front of Judge Johnson's bench so everyone in the courtroom could see the hoverboard that wouldn't fly. A monument to the scam perpetrated on 100,000 people.

"Why did you bring this lawsuit, Mr. Stubble?"

"Because the toy didn't work. I want my money back. But not just that. Companies who lie should be taught a lesson. It was a mean trick, leading me to believe I could fly. That thing right there," he said, pointing at the hoverboard, "never got off the ground."

"Terrible," Greenback said, "just terrible. Now then, Mr. Stubble, how did you realize you weren't alone?"

"I set up a Facebook page called Hoverboard Hades to blow off a little steam and the number of Likes I got on that page nearly crashed my computer. And the Likes just kept coming. Within a week, it was clear that thousands of people shelled out good money for a chance to fly and got nothing in return but a piece of painted fiberglass that won't move. I used that Facebook page to identify and survey the class members."

"Please explain."

"I thought it would be helpful to the court to have the class members answer a few questions. Better than having 100,000 people come to testify."

Judge Johnson nodded. Greenback was getting somewhere now.

"What were the questions?"

"Did you buy a Reindeer Hoverboard made by Tip Top Toy Company? Did it work? Do you want your money back? Do you want Tip Top Toy Company to be punished?"

"And what kind of response did you get?"

"Pretty good participation. One hundred percent. Answers were yes, no, yes and yes."

"Excuse me. One hundred thousand people said they bought the hoverboard, it didn't work, they want their money back and they want to see Tip Top Toy Company punished?"

"You got it," Stubble said. A cheer went up from the audience. When the noise died down, Greenback said, "no further questions."

Sarah Kennedy was on her feet. "Mr. Stubble, tell the court the questions you put on your survey about the warning label on the hoverboard."

"Excuse me?"

"Tell the court the questions you asked these 100,000 people about the warning label."

"I didn't ask any."

"What?" Sarah looked confused. "You didn't want to know if they read the warning label?"

"Nope. Didn't seem material to me."

Johnson smiled to himself. This witness was smarter than the doctor.

Greenback stood up. "Your honor, plaintiffs stipulate that they don't believe in Santa Claus and that they received and read the warning about True Believers. All of which is irrelevant."

"With that stipulation," Sarah said, "I just have a few more questions." Sarah proceeded to have Mr. Stubble repeat for Judge Johnson the helpful admissions he gave in his deposition and then ended her examination.

Johnson was perplexed. Did that mean defense counsel had a plan to prove the Reindeer Hoverboard actually works? He looked at the clock. "We'll break now," he said. "Be back at 2:00."

Same Day – 2:00 p.m.

Judge Johnson was ready for the next witness, and Tammy Brighthouse wasted no time accommodating him.

"State your name for the record."

"Paul Stancil Wingnut."

"It's Dr. Wingnut, correct?" She emphasized the word "doctor."

"Yes, ma'am. I have two Ph.D.s and a masters."

"My, my," Brighthouse said, "those are a lot of degrees."

"What can I say? I love learning," Wingnut said.

"You're to be commended," she said. "Please tell us about your degrees."

"I earned my doctorate degrees in psychology and statistics from Stanford and my master's degree in fantasy fiction from Not-True-U."

Johnson was confused. He held up his hand toward Brighthouse and asked Wingnut a question. "What is Not-True-U?"

"An online university, specializing in the study of how fantasy fiction affects human behavior."

"And how does your degree in fantasy fiction help in this case?" Judge Johnson asked, thinking he might like the answer.

"Fantasy fiction is like a drug. The more people consume it, the more they believe in it. Their minds often end up falling prey to fairy tales about magical beings," Wingnut said. "Like Santa Claus, for example."

"I see," Judge Johnson said. "You may proceed, Ms. Brighthouse."

"Impressive résumé," Brighthouse said. "What is your affiliation with the League of Informed Entrepreneurs?"

"I am the founder of LIE. I've put my life's work into it."

"Please tell the court about LIE."

"The League of Informed Entrepreneurs is here to protect businesses from major lies. We identify the lies that hurt business, report on them to the world and, if necessary, go to court to stop them."

"Is there a lie in this case you hope to stop?"

"Yes, ma'am. The Santa lie."

Brighthouse paused, looked around for effect and then asked, "The Santa lie?"

"Yes. The lie that Santa is real."

Judge Johnson's mood improved. It was about time plaintiffs used a witness who could put an end to this case.

Wingnut continued. "Lying to children is never good. It causes them to question authority and distrust the world around them. Our study has shown—"

"Excuse me, Dr. Wingnut," Brighthouse said. "Before we get to your study, is there a specific harm caused by the Santa lie that brings you here?"

"Yes, ma'am. Tip Top Toy Company's sale of The Reindeer Hoverboard."

"And how is that of interest to LIE?"

"It's a perfect example of false marketing using the Santa lie."

Brighthouse grabbed a large binder from the desk in front of her and held it up. "Which leads us to the study you mentioned."

"Yes, ma'am. About 20 years ago, we received a grant from an international toy company to study the harms caused to business by the Santa lie."

Johnson saw Raker whisper something to Kennedy, who made a note on her legal pad.

"Why did it take so long to complete the study?" Brighthouse asked.

"It was a condition of the study. Our benefactor said it had to be thorough, for at least 20 years, or the funding would stop."

Brighthouse approached the witness and had him explain the details of the study for Judge Johnson. This was great information. It would help his ruling. Johnson asked a few questions, just to be sure the record was clear. "This study is fully verified?"

"Yes, sir."

"Meets all requisite academic standards?"

"Absolutely."

"Smallest margin of error?"

"The smallest."

Johnson smiled and waved to Brighthouse to continue.

"There is something I don't understand, Dr. Wingnut," Brighthouse said. "How can it be bad for business for children to believe in Santa Claus?"

"Our study shows that even though parents engage in a steady flow of gift-buying from retailers for the few years when children believe in Santa, parents use the lie to save money at the store when their children stop believing. The years after the kids learn the truth are a shock to the economy."

"But if you convince all children not to believe in Santa Claus, won't that shock the economy more?"

"Not at all. Think about it. Parents love their children. They will give them gifts when they're young even if they don't believe in Santa. Our study followed a cohort of families whose children never believed and there was no decline in gift-buying for the children until the children turned 18. This created more business for retailers."

Judge Johnson interrupted again. "And your study proves this?"

"Yes, sir."

Brighthouse changed the focus to the harm to children. "How is it harmful for children to believe in Santa Claus?"

"The study shows that children who are told the truth by their parents at an early age have better relationships with their parents. They are more trusting, not always wondering in later years what other lies their parents told them."

Judge Johnson took the reins from Brighthouse.

"Dr. Wingnut, I can see you are well-qualified and you have spent many years researching this issue. What is it that you want this court to do?"

"LIE is asking you to enter an injunction that prevents Tip Top Toy Company from lying about the existence of Santa Claus. With your order, we'll take this fight to other jurisdictions and make the world a better place. Where truth matters. And where fantasy belongs in books."

"I think I've got it." Judge Johnson leaned back in his chair and swiveled in the direction of Sarah Kennedy. "Your turn."

Sarah Kennedy knew she'd have to tread lightly with Paul Stancil Wingnut, Ph.D.

"Dr. Wingnut, good afternoon."

"Afternoon, Ms. Kennedy."

"That grant you received 20 years ago to study the effect of believing in Santa Claus? You say it was funded by an international toy company? That wouldn't happen to be North Pole Enterprises, LLC, would it?"

"It would."

"Do you know Hank Snow?"

"I do. He's affiliated with North Pole Enterprises and is a member of LIE's Board of Directors."

"How fitting."

"Excuse me."

"Did you know that Hank Snow is in jail on federal felony charges?"

Wingnut looked to Brighthouse for help. "I didn't know that."

"Is he the example of the type of board member LIE seeks?" Sarah asked.

"Objection," Brighthouse said, "argumentative."

"What's your point, Ms. Kennedy?" Judge Johnson asked.

"Credibility of the report, your honor. I can close the gap."

"Do it quickly."

"Dr. Wingnut, did you know that at the time North Pole Enterprises funded LIE's study of Santa Claus, Hank Snow had just tried to interfere in the trial of a man named Henry Edmonds by claiming that Santa Claus is not real? And that he continued to try to do so in a subsequent trial?"

"Doesn't sound like interference to me."

"You gave Hank Snow exactly what he wanted, didn't you?"

"I don't follow," Wingnut said.

"Hank Snow has never acknowledged in public that Santa Claus is real."

"Sounds like a stable person."

"He funded LIE's study," Sarah said, "because he knew what the outcome would be. He knew you would find that believing in Santa Claus causes dire consequences."

"Are you challenging the academic integrity of LIE's study?"

"That's exactly what I'm doing, Dr. Wingnut. When you took the money, did you believe in Santa Claus?"

"Of course not."

"So, you based your study on a hypothesis you didn't test?" Sarah asked.

"Well, I—"

"True or false, Dr. Wingnut. You did nothing to determine whether Santa Claus is real?"

"Objection," Brighthouse shouted.

"Ms. Kennedy," Judge Johnson said, "Do I need to order your medical examination next?"

"The question, your honor, is whether the study meets the academic rigor that is required. May I continue?"

Judge Johnson looked uncertain but he let her continue.

"Dr. Wingnut, did you or did you not do anything to determine whether Santa Claus is real?"

"No, I didn't." Wingnut smirked.

"That was just a conclusion you reached without any scientific analysis of Santa's existence?"

Wingnut looked at Sarah as if a trap were being set. Sarah prodded him again: "Can you answer the question?"

"That's true. There was no scientific analysis."

Sarah stood up and faced Judge Johnson. "Your honor, we move to strike the testimony of Dr. Wingnut. He is offering an opinion that is not based on scientific work. His expert opinion is unsubstantiated. I have several precedents I can present to the court prohibiting such testimony."

Both Brighthouse and Greenback were on their feet complaining. "This is a lawyer's trick," Greenback shouted. Brighthouse was quick to add, "The question of Santa's existence does not need to be scientifically tested in a rational society."

Judge Johnson looked displeased with Sarah Kennedy. "I had expected this from your husband, but not you. Your motion is denied. Do you have any more questions?"

"Judge Johnson, in the Twirly Masters trial, you disputed the existence of Santa Claus and the jury came back for the other side. I submit that—"

"You will submit no such thing. You're about to cross the line."

Sarah knew she had done as much damage as she could to Wingnut's credibility and Johnson wasn't having it. Perhaps the next line of questions would help with Austin Land's social-media campaign.

"Dr. Wingnut, one of the other fights that LIE has been waging the last 20 years has to do with the subject of global warming, correct?"

"Yes, but I'm not the primary authority for that."

"You're the founder of LIE. Surely, you have knowledge of LIE's position on the subject."

"Well, sure. Global warming is a hoax, and the lie hurts business. Simple as that."

"Dr. Wingnut," Sarah said, "isn't it true that the ice sheet at the North Pole is melting at an alarming rate?"

"Not true."

"Dr. Wingnut, if you're wrong about that fact and wrong about the existence of Santa Claus, then Santa's village is at risk, isn't it?"

Wingnut laughed. "Okay, I'll play along. Yes, if I'm wrong, rising temperatures will wipe out Santa's village."

Sarah could hear the tapping of Austin Land's computer behind her, probably wrapping up his story for the afternoon social-media push.

"That would be your expert opinion, Dr. Wingnut?" She emphasized the word "expert."

"Sure," he said. "My expert opinion."

Sarah turned around to see Austin Land holding his phone and thumbing away. He was probably sending tweets to Santa's followers and pictures to Santa's Instagram account. Good. "No further questions."

Same Day – 4:30 p.m.

The helicopter thumped down on the hard-packed ice and its rotors started to wind down. Liz, Twirly, Henry and Mistletoe unbuckled their seatbelts and donned their gloves, face protection and headwear. The temperature outside was minus-10 Fahrenheit.

Liz peered out her window, but couldn't see much. Twenty-four hour darkness was the norm this time of year. She knew from her research that they had just touched down on the Greenland ice sheet in the northeastern segment of Greenland National Park, the largest protected park in the world. The park had no permanent residents. Liz hoped to change that soon.

Henry opened the door and stepped to the ground. Liz and the others followed. The headlights on the chopper shined a path toward a small building that looked like a poor imitation of an ice-fishing shack.

"That's where we're going," Mistletoe said.

Just inside the front door was a set of steps. Only one way to go. Down.

"Follow me," Mistletoe said.

Liz could hear a low hum once they were below ground. "What's that noise?"

"The generator," Mistletoe said. "Keeps the lights on."

For the next hour, the elf guided Liz, Twirly and Henry through a maze of underground tunnels. Liz thought it looked just like the pictures Tarina had shown her, only sharper. The walls of ice in the tunnels had a shine to them and had been reinforced with wooden beams and roughhewn plank floors. All the tunnel walls had wooden railings. Liz wondered where they'd found the timber. As if reading her mind, Mistletoe said, "The wooden beams and floorboards were shipped from locations around the world."

Along the tunnels were doors to more than 30 underground rooms. Mistletoe showed them one of the mess halls, complete with 500 elf-sized picnic tables, and one of the barracks, with 1,500 bunk beds, any one of which would fit Mistletoe perfectly. The records room had a cavernous safe for important documents, and the manufacturing rooms had workbenches stocked with tools along all the walls. Distribution occupied five enormous rooms tied together by conveyor belts and with scaffolds to hold the presents.

"As you can see," Mistletoe offered, "it's just about ready."

"Can you show me the core samples?" Liz asked.

"Sure thing," she said. "Follow me."

A few minutes later, they came to a room with "Research" painted on the door. Mistletoe showed the way and pointed to a wall-mounted row of 30 glass cabinets holding core samples taken by the elves. Liz took her time examining the core samples. The computer printouts Lucky had shown her were attached to each cabinet.

"What do you think?" Mistletoe asked, after Liz was finished. "Will the underground village last?" Twirly and Henry were standing next to her, looking hopefully at Liz.

"Tarina selected a good site for the village and Lucky paid close attention to details in the construction." Liz said. "There is a risk the ice will shift, but it will work this year, and we can put in a battery-operated safety system to monitor any future changes in the ice sheet. I'd say that all we need now are some tenants."

"Yes!" Mistletoe said, jumping up to slap high fives with Twirly and Henry. "I knew it."

During the celebration, Liz's satellite phone buzzed. She picked it up, listened, and before she hung up, said, "Don't worry. I'll get there somehow."

"What's wrong?" Henry asked.

"That was Holly," Liz said. "Cane moved her hearing up to early tomorrow morning. He wants to banish her before I get there. I told her not to worry, but I'm not sure how I will get there in time."

"Travel by boat will take too long. Yes, indeed," Twirly said.

"I have an idea," Mistletoe said. "Follow me." She led everyone through a tunnel that ended at a set of stairs. "Up and out."

She ran up the stairs and pushed the door open. Two lanterns provided minimal light to the area they entered. They were under a pitched roof, with solid wooden crossbeams halfway up, bracing the

174

sides of a small building. Liz immediately took in the scent of hay and manure. When her eyes adjusted to her shadowed surroundings, she realized she was standing in the middle of a set of stalls. Something bumped her in the back and startled her. She turned around to find herself face to face with a large reindeer, whose head stuck out over the half door to one of the building's stalls.

"Meet Lightning," Mistletoe said. "Part of the reindeer backup team that will fly you to the North Pole."

"Marvelous," Twirly said. "Just marvelous, indeed."

"What? With who? You?"

Mistletoe laughed. "No, I'm just the hostler for these fine animals and I look nothing like Santa Claus. You can't have a backup reindeer team without a backup Santa Claus. Who do you know in this room who looks like Santa?" Mistletoe nodded toward Henry and smiled.

Liz said to Henry, "Backup Santa, huh?"

"It's like being a teacher who drives the school bus part-time," Henry said. "Just a way to pick up some extra spending money."

"He's too modest," Mistletoe said. "During the Christmas of '64, hail pelted Santa's sleigh over

England, rendering it inoperable. Henry took over and made the remaining deliveries before morning. And then there was the—"

Henry interrupted. "That's enough, Mistletoe. We don't have much time." Looking at Liz, he said, "How would you like to go on the ride of a lifetime?"

Wednesday, December 19ᵗʰ

At promptly 7 a.m., the chamber door to the Elf High Council opened and a brutish elf wearing a sergeant-at-arms badge filled the door frame and made himself known in a loud voice. "The banishment hearing will commence in three minutes. If you are Holly the Elf or her representative, draw near and be heard. All others are excluded, by order of Chairman Zachary Cane."

Liz and Holly were the only ones in the hallway. They got up and followed the sergeant-at-arms.

"Take off your hat," the sergeant-at-arms barked at Holly.

177

Holly pulled her trademark headgear off of her head, folded the ball cap and stuck it into her back pocket.

When they entered the chamber, Liz could hear the low hum coming from beyond the walls, the village's manufacturing machinery at work. The next thing she noticed was the low lighting in the room. She could barely make out four figures behind the bench 30 yards in the distance. There were plenty of pews on each side of the aisle, but the seats were empty. Liz and Holly walked the distance down the aisle and took their places at a metal table in the center of the room facing the Elf High Council. The four figures looked down on them. There was only one friendly face: Snowflake's.

"So, you made it, did you?" Cane had his elbows on the bench. His forefingers touched his sharp nose while his protruding chin rested on his thumbs. His eyes were hard to see, because they were in shadow. Like the room itself.

"Yes, sir, I made it," Liz said. "I'm here as Holly's representative."

"You want to play lawyer, do you? Be like your father? Save someone?"

Liz didn't answer. She could feel the sarcasm in his voice. Snowflake came to her rescue. "Mr. Chairman, sir, shall we get on with the hearing?"

Cane glanced at Snowflake. "Very well. Let's proceed with the reading of the charges." He nodded to one of the old elves next to him, who took out a scroll, unrolled it and began to read.

"Holly the Elf is charged with violating Elf High Council Edict 1983, which makes clear that there is no such thing as global warming and all research on the subject is banned. To wit: she wrongfully engaged in clandestine research, drilling without a license and stirring up lies that the North Pole ice sheet is melting. The penalty for these charges is banishment for life."

"How do you plead?" Cane asked Holly. "Guilty or not guilty?"

Before Holly could answer, the low hum that served as white noise in the room stopped. Liz knew this was coming. It was part of the plan. The quiet that followed was what was left after the manufacturing machinery came to a halt. Since the machines ran 364 days out of the year, it was a startling development to some of the members of the council. Liz could see the nervous looks on their faces, all except one: Snowflake's. A grin appeared there.

"Sergeant-at-arms," Cane said, "find out what happened." He added, "Now."

The big elf hustled down the aisle to the main door and when he unlocked and opened it, a crowd of elves half his size greeted him. Before he could stop them, they flowed around him like water skirting a piling in the ocean surf. There was nothing he could do to hold back the flow. And they just kept coming.

Liz felt more confident as the massive room filled to capacity with Holly's friends. Soon, all the seats were taken.

"Everyone out," Cane shouted, but no one moved. "I can have you all banished." He waved his arms to take in the whole room.

"Excuse me, Mr. Chairman," Snowflake offered, "but if you banish everyone, how will you manage the logistics of Christmas? You won't have anyone to do the work."

"This is an illegal union strike," Cane said. "I have the power to discipline even if I don't banish."

"Why not let them attend?" Snowflake asked. "Show the elf community that you're not afraid for justice to occur in the open. If you have enough evidence to banish Holly, everyone will see it for themselves and you will avoid rumors."

Liz watched Cane's reaction. His face did not betray his thoughts. If he felt trapped, he didn't show it.

"Fine. I order everyone to stay," he said to the room at large, "and witness what happens when you defy an edict of the Elf High Council." He then looked directly at Holly. "What is your plea?"

Liz placed her hand on Holly's shoulder to have her wait. "Point of order," she said.

"What is it?" Cane snapped.

"We challenge the Sanstitutionality of the edict." Liz had done her homework. When Santa set up shop at the North Pole with Cane's permission, Santa and Cane adopted a Sanstitution. It was similar in concept to the American Constitution, and had a Bill of Rights that afforded basic protections to North Pole citizens.

"On what grounds are you challenging Edict 1983?"

Liz wanted to say "stupidity," but she held her tongue. "The edict makes an unscientific conclusion about global warming and prevents scientific research on the topic. Article 12 of the Bill of Rights provides that all legislation to banish an elf must be in furtherance of the safety and operation of the North Pole."

"So what?" Cane said. "What does global warming have to do with the safety of the North Pole?"

The expression on Cane's face showed he recognized his mistake as soon as he finished his question. For the next hour, Liz spoke with a strong, confident voice on the science of global warming, and how the reality of the situation was closing in on the North Pole.

"The outside temperature this morning was just above freezing," Liz said. "It's alarming." She had recent temperature and sea-level data for the Arctic region, and with Holly's help, she had the local core sample data. She gave it all to the Council.

At several times during Liz's speech, Cane tried to interrupt, but she'd read the Council's procedural rules and used them to regain her footing.

"The threat is real," Liz concluded. Turning around to face the crowd of concerned faces, she said, "I give it two weeks, at most."

"Look at us when addressing the Council," Cane demanded. "What do you give two weeks?"

"The stability of the ice we're standing on."

The elves started to mutter among themselves.

Liz continued. "It could be sooner, but when it happens, it will be quick. The ice will shift like plates beneath the earth colliding in an earthquake. Cracks will develop. They will get larger by the second. Water will start to pour in. The buildings will flood, break apart and disappear below the surface. All the presents for this year's Christmas will be lost."

"No," one elf in the audience cried out.

"It can't be," another cried.

"But that's not the worst part," Liz said. "The lives of everyone at the North Pole could be lost. And it will be the end of Christmas, forever."

When she stopped, she thought she'd never heard a silence as deep and clear as the one that surrounded her.

Cane leaned toward the two Council elves sitting at his right and whispered to them. They nodded. Snowflake tried to get Cane's attention but he waved her away. He turned back to face Liz and said, "Your challenge to Edict 1983 is rejected. We—"

Snowflake interrupted, "I vote otherwise, sir."

"No matter," Cane said. "It's time to move on. How do you plead, Holly the Elf?"

Liz looked to Holly, who seemed nervous but ready. "I take full responsibility for trying to protect the North Pole, to research the risks to it and to warn the elves before it's too late."

"Meaning," Cane said, "you plead guilty to violating Edict 1983. In that case, you're banished for life from the North Pole, effective immediately. Remove yourself from this chamber, collect your belongings and be gone within the hour. Take your friend," he pointed at Liz, "with you."

Liz heard the main door open and loud murmuring from the audience at the far end of the chamber. She turned toward the sound to see a tall, fit woman with hair as white as snow, striding toward her. The woman wore black, tight-fitting jeans, a red top and white vest.

"Who is that?" Liz whispered to Holly.

"Mrs. Claus."

"But I thought—"

"The make-believe images in books are way off," Holly said.

"She looks like Tarina."

"Just as strong-willed, too. Probably more so."

When Mrs. Claus arrived at the table where Liz and Holly sat, she leaned over and put her hand on Holly's shoulder. "You are a brave little elf, Holly. Thank you." She stood up and turned to Liz. "Santa Claus and I have been watching this proceeding on computerized live-stream. We are proud of you. Time I stepped in to help."

"What are you doing here?" Cane said to Mrs. Claus.

"Santa sent me as his designee. Have you forgotten that this is a two-branch system of government? The Elf High Council controls the operational side. You get to make laws and issue judgments, but Santa controls the inspirational side. He can confer gifts, and one of those gifts is in Article 20 of the Bill of Rights."

"Let me guess," Cane said to Mrs. Claus. "You intend to exercise Santa's authority to pardon Holly the Elf."

"I do."

"You realize this is the first time Santa has exercised that right since the founding of the North Pole government."

"It's about time. He would have done it when you banned Tarina if there had been a similar threat to the North Pole. Holly is pardoned so she can continue her work on the Santa Relocation Plan."

Cane placed his elbows on the bench, his nose against his forefingers and his thumbs under his chin. "My security team alerted me to this Santa Relocation Plan. Totally unnecessary," he said. "Global warming is a hoax. Fake news. Media gone crazy. Not to be trusted. Left-wing scientists at work."

Cane waved the sergeant-at-arms forward to the bench and whispered something to him. The large elf hustled out the side door as Cane said, "For the protection of the village, I'm calling out the Elf National Guard. It will blockade the ice sheet," Cane said. "Nothing coming in or going out, except necessities and Christmas supplies. Everyone will be protected."

"That's not protection," Mrs. Claus said. "You're dooming Santa's village to destruction and endangering the lives of its inhabitants. You're going to end Christmas forever."

"I disagree," Cane said. "This is just a cycle. We will have some melting, but the snow and freezing will return."

Liz thought about the shocking document Snowflake had given her when Henry dropped her off at the North Pole in the middle of the night. "This is what Hank Snow stole from the White House," Snowflake had said to her. "You may need to use it if Cane won't listen to reason. Keep it to yourself for now."

"I know why you're doing this," Liz said to Cane. "It's because of the document Hank Snow sent you."

Cane's face drew tight with anger. "Not another word from you, Liz Raker. That's top secret." He turned to look at Snowflake, disgust written on his face.

One of the elves in the audience yelled, "Tell us." Another asked, "Is it about global warming?"

The door to Cane's right opened and a line of tall, strong-looking elves entered the room at a trot and formed a line in front of the Elf High Council. They wore green flannel pants, white shirts and red suspenders and carried shields in the shape of stockings and wooden batons like candy canes. Behind them came more ENG members, with more shields and batons. Half of them peeled off down one side of the chamber and half down the other side. The audience of working-class elves got quiet. The Elf National Guard had them surrounded.

"Everyone must leave this room and get back to work," Cane said. He stood with his palms resting on the bench in front of him and leaned in to make his point. "Now."

The elves silently made their way down the center aisle and out the doorway. They looked defeated. When they were gone, Mrs. Claus stepped forward. "You have no right to use the Elf National Guard in this way." Liz and Holly stood with her, showing their support.

Cane ignored the rebuke. He sat down and said, "Now what is it you think you know, Liz Raker?"

"You wrongly accused Hank Snow of treason after he found a document at the White House confirming a conspiracy between the United States,

Russia and China to mine minerals at the North Pole." Liz looked at Holly and Mrs. Claus and saw the surprise in their faces. Apparently, Snowflake had not shared this information with them.

"Pure conjecture on your part." Cane wasn't about to admit anything.

"If it's conjecture," Liz said, "why are you determined to ignore the reality of global warming?" He started to respond, but Liz answered her own question. "It's because you want those governments to pay you to leave. If you depart voluntarily, you abandon your stake and they won't have to pay you. They'll just take what's left."

"There's no reason to leave the village," Cane said.

"Not true," Liz said. "The document shows that these governments have been engaged in a plan for the past 20 years to accelerate the environmental disaster at the North Pole by chipping away at environmental protection regulations in their countries. You've been using this document to blackmail the three most powerful countries in the world. They either pay what you want or you release the document to the public. You've been endangering the lives of everyone in the village because of your greed."

Mrs. Claus walked toward the line of national guard elves between her and Cane. She put her hands on the shoulders of the two elves in the middle of the line and pushed them aside. They looked uncertain about whether to resist, but then opened a path for her. She stepped closer to the bench and looked up at Cane. "I always suspected you were a selfish elf. You never cared about Christmas. That was clear when you banished my daughter, Tarina. You never knew what happened to her, did you?"

"I don't care where she went."

"She became our contingency plan against you. Over the last 150 years, half our Christmas output has come from a company she and I founded, together." Mrs. Claus folded her arms and leaned back, with a sly smile on her face. "So, you see, Zachary Cane, you don't control the operations of Christmas as much as you thought you did."

Cane stood up and looked down at Mrs. Claus. "I suspected there was treasonous activity by Tarina Winter but I could never prove it. Thanks for the admission. As for things I control," he said. "I control what goes on in this village. Effective immediately, you, Liz Raker and Holly are confined to your quarters until Christmas. For your own good," he added. "Guards, escort them out of here and confiscate their cellphones, computers and other communication devices. We don't want them making contact with the outside world until the deal is done."

"The deal?" Mrs. Claus said.

"Yes." Cane laughed. "Liz Raker was right. The sale of the North Pole closes on Christmas Eve. China, Russia and the United States have been trying to lowball me, but thanks to Hank Snow, I now have the evidence—the document—to make them pay what I deserve. If they don't pay me, the whole world learns how these governments conspired to sacrifice the environment for selfish profit." Cane laughed again. "The politicians thought they could sink me and grab the spoils, but I have the trump card for a big payday."

"You're admitting your treachery in front of the ENG?"

"I'm cutting them in."

"And the rest of the Council?"

"These two are with me," Cane said, pointing to his right. Turning to Snowflake, he said, "By the way, you're confined to The Archives until this is done. If all goes according to plan, you and everyone else can leave the next day. As for Hank Snow, he's a traitor. He can rot in jail."

Liz moved forward. "And if I'm right and Santa's village collapses before Christmas Eve?"

"Then you will go down with the rest of us." Cane stood. "Guards, take them. I have business to attend."

Liz saw Snowflake hurriedly type something on her phone just before one of the guards grabbed it.

Same Day – 9:30 a.m.

Tarina Winter stepped from the police van and walked to the back door of the courthouse for Day 2 of the hearing in the hoverboard case, her escort by her side. Judge Johnson approached from another part of the secure parking area. They met at the back door.

"Welcome back," he said. "I hope you enjoyed your accommodations last night." Tarina thought he appeared to be too satisfied with her situation. A course correction was in order.

"It had your touch," she said. "Bland, dark, cold and, of course, dense."

Johnson's eyes narrowed. "Do you want another 24 hours?"

"Sure," Tarina said, holding her hands above her head in the surrender position. "Let's put this off another day."

"You'd like that, wouldn't you?" Johnson said. "Delaying judgment. Not in my courtroom. This case ends today." He stomped off.

When Tarina entered the courtroom, it was filled to capacity. The rowdy crowd on the plaintiff side of the courtroom, who had booed her the day before, welcomed her back by chanting "liar" in steady, humming tones. But there also was a new, younger group, who'd commandeered the defense side of the courtroom. Most looked like college students and many wore shirts featuring environmental commentary. Her favorite was "Save the whales. Teach Santa to swim." Raker waved her over to where he and Sarah were standing.

"I see we have a few supporters," Tarina said.

Raker laughed. "Looks like Austin Land's media campaign was a success. They came early, filled this side of the courtroom and prevented a contingent of LIE supporters from getting seats. The overflow support from both sides have planted themselves on the lawn out front with dueling protest signs. The media are loving it."

"So, what's next?" Tarina asked.

"You are," Sarah said. "You ready?"

"Just cover the basics and turn me over to the other side. I'll take it from there," Tarina said.

Judge Johnson entered the courtroom in a hurry. When the bailiff finished with his "oyez, oyez" routine, Johnson looked at the lawyers and said, "Who's next?"

Tarina was on her feet before she was announced. She rounded her end of the defense table and strode toward the witness box. She stopped in the middle of the courtroom to look at the Reindeer Hoverboard that was leaning against Judge Johnson's bench. She walked up to it and gave it a nudge to straighten it. When she did, the lights came on and the toy emitted a low hum.

"What's that?" Judge Johnson said.

"Reindeer Hoverboard," Tarina said. "Seems to be working fine." She walked over, took the oath, took her seat and crossed her legs.

"Ms. Winter," Sarah asked, "can you tell the court how long Tip Top Toy Company has been in business?"

"One hundred fifty years."

"How did the company choose Greenland for its headquarters?"

"The climate." Looking at Judge Johnson, Tarina added, "And the judges. They're much nicer than the ones here." Judge Johnson stopped writing on his pad and turned his head. Tarina noticed that Sarah quickened the pace of her questions.

"Ms. Winter, has Tip Top Toy Company ever been sued for product liability?"

"This is the first time."

"That's a remarkable record," Sarah said.

"It'd be perfect if it weren't for this frivolous case."

"Objection," Greenback said.

"Sustained." Judge Johnson was stern. "Ms. Winter, confine yourself to the facts."

"You mean like the fact that this entire hearing is a sham? A way to keep my case from the jury?"

"Enough." Judge Johnson was holding his gavel.

"Please be careful with that," Tarina said. "Last time you got excited with that thing, you put a dent in the judge's face on the wall behind you. I don't want to be the next victim." Judge Johnson's mouth fell open. Tarina heard Sarah's next question before he could say anything.

"Ms. Winter, let's discuss the Reindeer Hoverboard. Where was it manufactured?"

"The prototype was made at our plant in Greenland. We used two other locations to complete the work."

"Were there any problems with the manufacturing process?"

"None whatsoever."

"Were the hoverboards tested before they were shipped to customers?"

"Every one of them."

"And?"

"They were all fine. We have extensive records to prove it."

"What do you have to say to the plaintiffs in this case?"

"Which ones?"

"Let's start with LIE."

"Great name for them," Tarina said.

"Objection," Brighthouse said. "That's opinion. Not fact."

Tarina Winter leaned forward and said, "That's exactly my opinion, Tammy. Your client lies better than a well-trained shyster."

"Move to strike, your honor." Tammy Brighthouse flushed. Tarina enjoyed the reaction.

"I agree," Tarina said. "Let's strike LIE's unscientific opinion about global warming and their patronizing opinions about children and adults who believe in Santa Claus."

"Sustained," Judge Johnson said. "The objection is sustained."

"Thank you," Tarina said.

"That was not for you," he said to Tarina. She thought his face would cave in on itself.

Tarina had a good response but Sarah threw her a question first. "Ms. Winter, LIE says global warming is made up. Do you agree?"

"They've never been to Greenland then. The next largest ice sheet in the world after the Antarctic and melting faster than his patience." She tilted her head to indicate the judge.

"And what about the psychological effect on children believing in Santa Claus? LIE says it's a problem."

"What's wrong with children believing in Santa Claus?" She brushed a lock of her silver-gray hair away from her left eye. "Just because ambulance chasers, profiteering interest groups and incompetent judges don't believe in Santa, that's no reason to pick on the kids. All the children I've ever known who believed in Santa Claus have turned out just fine." Tarina looked at Judge Johnson as she added, "Except perhaps for a few."

"That's all we have, your honor," Sarah said. Tarina turned toward the plaintiffs. Time for the fun to begin, she thought.

Greenback went first. "Ms. Winter, you say there is nothing wrong with the Reindeer Hoverboard?"

"That's right. It works just fine."

"Permission to perform a demonstration, your honor?"

"Granted, but make it quick."

Greenback walked over to the hoverboard leaning against Judge Johnson's bench. He picked it up and laid it on the floor. Then he stepped on top of it, the weight of his large frame pressing it into the floor. Nothing happened.

"Ms. Winter," he said, "as you can see, the Reindeer Hoverboard doesn't work."

"Maybe you're too heavy."

"Funny, Ms. Winter, but wrong answer. It's not making a sound."

Tarina turned to the judge. "Permission to put him in his place?"

Before Judge Johnson could answer, Tarina bolted from the witness box and made her way to where Greenback stood on the hoverboard. She knelt down and placed her right hand on the back of the board. The lights around the edge came on and the board began to hum. Vibrations followed. A few seconds later, the hoverboard began to lift off the ground. Greenback raised his arms and bent his knees in an effort to balance. Coordination did not appear to be one of his talents. He inhaled deeply and looked down in shock as the board lifted a foot off the ground; it began to wobble under his 320-pound frame. Judge Johnson rose out of his chair and leaned forward to see what was happening.

"How's that for not working?" Tarina said to Greenback, in a way that made it appear the question was directed at the entire courtroom. No one answered.

The board rose higher in the air and as it did, Tarina got to her feet, still gripping the back of the hoverboard. It leveled off at about three feet above the ground. Greenback was hardly breathing now, sweat beading on his brow as he tried to balance in midair, looking directly at a surprised Judge Johnson. Tarina looked around to see people in the audience standing to get a better look. She noticed Austin Land in one corner recording the scene with his phone.

"Shut it off," Greenback said, as he swayed back and forth to keep from falling.

"Are you sure?" Tarina asked.

"Your honor?" Greenback pleaded.

"Ms. Winter," Judge Johnson said, "I order you to shut that thing off."

Tarina took her right hand off the back of the hoverboard. The lights went off. The humming stopped. And Greenback came tumbling down, landing hard on his back when he hit the ground. When he rolled to his side, he looked more like a dead walrus than a live ambulance chaser. Tarina stepped over him without a care for his condition and walked back to the witness box. The bailiffs rushed to help Greenback.

"Are you all right, Mr. Greenback?" Judge Johnson inquired.

Greenback groaned.

"I think he hurt his back," one of the bailiffs said.

"Do you have no shame, woman?" Judge Johnson asked. "Look what you've done."

"You ordered me to shut it off."

Johnson's eyes darted back and forth between Tarina and Greenback. The bailiffs helped Greenback to his feet and served as crutches, one on each arm, as he returned to his seat. "Do you need a break, Mr. Greenback?"

Greenback leaned over to Brighthouse and whispered to her before replying, "No, your honor.

Ms. Brighthouse will take over from here." He grunted as he said the word "here."

Brighthouse didn't hesitate. "Ms. Winter, that was quite a show."

"Would you like a ride, too?" Tarina asked. A few audience members laughed. Judge Johnson scowled at them.

Brighthouse dodged the quip. "Please tell the court how you pulled off that trick, how you made a defective hoverboard fly."

"Here and here," Tarina said. She pointed to her head, and then to her heart.

"I don't follow," Brighthouse said.

"I didn't expect you would, Tammy. You never believed, even as a little girl."

"Ah," Brighthouse said, "so the reason the hoverboard worked is because you believe in Santa Claus."

"I'm glad you're coming around."

Brighthouse turned to face Judge Johnson. "Your honor, we move that the entire testimony of this witness be stricken from the record. She's incompetent. Claims Santa Claus is real. Wastes the court's time. Judgment should be entered for the plaintiffs without further delay."

Judge Johnson looked at Sarah. "She has a point."

Tarina didn't wait for her attorney to speak. "The hoverboard works, judge. Everyone saw it."

"She's right, your honor," Sarah said. "The plaintiffs want you to rule that the Reindeer Hoverboard is defective. It's not."

"But it didn't work for plaintiffs," Brighthouse said.

"Because they don't believe," Tarina said, "which proves I'm right and the plaintiffs are wrong."

Judge Johnson was scratching his chin, seemingly flustered by this development. "I'm going to let the witness continue to testify, but I reserve the right to strike her testimony later and rule against defendant."

Brighthouse picked up the study that Dr. Wingnut had testified about and handed it to Tarina. "Are you familiar with this study? It was funded by North Pole Enterprises."

Tarina flipped through it and recognized it as something her brother would sponsor. He had always tried to keep secrets, especially about Santa Claus.

"I disagree with the findings in this study," Tarina said.

"You don't think there is anything strange about adults who believe in Santa Claus?" Brighthouse asked.

"Only a small percentage of the adult population believes in Santa," Tarina said. "That makes them special, not strange. You, the judge and Mr. Bad Back there," she said, pointing to Greenback, "fall into the category of common thinkers who have no ability to believe."

Brighthouse raised her voice. "Santa Claus and global warming. Those are your beliefs."

"Yes, Tammy," Tarina said. Leaning forward, she added, "Did it ever occur to you that there is a connection between the two?"

"What are you talking about?" Brighthouse asked. She looked genuinely interested in the answer to the question.

"Why do you think Santa chose coal to give Naughty children?"

"I don't understand," Brighthouse said.

"Santa predicted the effects of the 20th century on the environment," Tarina said. "He knew before the scientists did that carbon dioxide released from the burning of fossil fuels—coal in particular—leads to global warming. If you want to make someone hate coal, give it to them as a gift for Christmas."

"You're saying that Santa—"

"Yes. Santa has been conditioning children to hate coal. Too bad he couldn't give them gasoline, too."

It took Brighthouse a moment to collect her thoughts. "Assuming there is a Santa Claus," Brighthouse said, "why would he care about global warming? He's at the North Pole. It's plenty cold there."

"As a matter of fact," Tarina said, "the North Pole ice sheet is melting, thanks to global warming. There's not much time left."

"Well, then," Brighthouse said, laughing, "we'd better wrap this up so you can go help Santa."

"I agree."

Judge Johnson looked at Tarina and shook his head. She looked back and shook hers, too. Brighthouse went over and picked up the hoverboard. She looked more confident as she pointed to the writing on the back. "Your warning on the Reindeer Hoverboard includes the words True Believers, correct?"

"It does."

"But the words True Believers are not defined anywhere in your literature, are they?"

Tarina groaned inwardly. This was the question she hoped would not be asked. She didn't have a good answer. Better to move along. "That's right."

"You can't find the term in the dictionary, can you?"

"No."

"In fact, you never informed purchasers anywhere in your warnings that adults needed to believe in Santa Claus for the hoverboard to work, did you?"

"I suppose that's right. We didn't mention Santa Claus."

"They had no way of knowing they needed to believe in Santa Claus for the hoverboard to work, did they?"

"Perhaps not, but—"

"No 'buts,' Ms. Winter."

Tarina stood up. "If they had believed, we wouldn't be here."

"Ms. Winter, you sold plaintiffs a hoverboard without fully disclosing how it works. That's deception. Its fraud." Brighthouse sat down with a smile on her face. Greenback patted her shoulder with his right hand while holding his back with his left. The audience on plaintiffs' side of the courtroom burst into applause.

"Let's take a 15-minute recess," Judge Johnson said. He got up and left the room. Tarina thought she caught a smile on his face as he turned away.

Same Day – 10:30 a.m.

The defense team found a small room next to the courtroom to talk strategy before Hank Snow testified. Raker was worried about their chances of success.

"I didn't help our case much at the end, did I?" Tarina asked.

"It couldn't be helped," Raker said. "They finally focused on our weak spot."

Tarina looked at Sarah. "How weak is our weak spot?"

"Our defense is based on the True Believers warning," Sarah said. "Judge Johnson has been looking for a way out. The lack of specificity in the warning may be his ticket."

"What now?" Tarina asked.

"The only witness left is Hank Snow," Sarah said. "Do you think there is any chance he will support you?"

"He and I had a chat at the jail," Tarina said. "I don't know what he will do."

This was news to Raker, but it explained why Tarina was so interested in getting herself locked up. "You aren't telling us everything you know about Hank Snow, are you?" Raker asked.

Tarina's phone buzzed. She ignored Raker's question as she answered the call.

"Twirly, what's going on?" She looked at Raker and Sarah as she listened. "Okay, thanks. Send me a copy of the text."

"What's the problem?" Sarah asked.

"Twirly and Henry haven't heard from anyone, including Liz, about Holly's hearing. All they got was a strange text from Snowflake. They can't reach any of them and they're worried something is wrong."

Tarina's phone buzzed again. It was Snowflake's text, forwarded by Twirly.

"What does the text say?" Raker asked. He feared for his daughter.

"It says, 'Hearing over. Village on lockdown. Cane conspiring. White House document. End near.'"

"What do you make of it, Tarina?" Sarah asked. She moved closer to Raker and took his hand.

"I don't know what Cane is conspiring to do or what the White House has to do with it, but a lockdown means no one can leave the North Pole, including Liz."

"What about 'end near'? What do you think that means?" Sarah asked.

"I think it means the ice is melting fast," Tarina said. Her face was grim.

While Raker considered the idea of his daughter being trapped on a sheet of ice about to collapse, there was a knock at the door. It was Austin Land. He asked to speak with Raker alone.

"Liz will be okay, Thad," Sarah said. "She is with Snowflake and Holly. We'll see you back in the courtroom." She kissed his cheek, and left with Tarina. Raker asked Land what this was about.

Land held out an envelope. "Someone handed this to me in the hallway and asked me to deliver it to you right away. Said it was for your eyes only."

It was addressed to Raker but there was no identification on the envelope as to whom it was from. Raker remembered the anonymous document he received during the Edmonds trial. He later learned that Hank Snow had delivered that document. He opened the envelope and read what was inside.

These papers didn't look like they came from Hank Snow. There was a cover memo and a legal document, neither of which helped Snow. When Raker finished reading, he was glad he finally had something useful. Snow himself, not Tip Top Toy Company, was the reason the hoverboard failed to fly.

Same Day – 10:45 a.m.

An officer from the county jail brought Hank Snow to the courtroom. Unlike Tarina Winter, who had served her brief sentence in jail, Snow was still in custody, facing felony criminal charges.

"What about the handcuffs, your honor?" the jailor asked.

"Mr. Snow," Judge Johnson said, "are you going to try to make a break for it?"

Snow looked around. The courtroom was guarded by a heavyset bailiff in one corner working a crossword puzzle. Another, standing near him, was trying to figure out how to loosen the belt around his waist.

"Doubt I'd have much chance against the elite force you've assembled," Snow said.

Johnson frowned but nodded. "Release him."

Snow caught Raker looking at him. This was the third time Raker would cross-examine him in court. Snow hadn't fared well the first two times. Maybe this time he would get what he wanted.

After Snow was sworn in, Judge Johnson looked at Greenback and asked, "Are you able to proceed?" Greenback winced as he shifted in his chair, holding his back, but said he would give it a go.

"Mr. Snow," Greenback said, "are you—"

"For the record," a voice behind Raker said. It was Judge Stark.

"What is it?" Judge Johnson snapped.

"I object to any question that has to do with Mr. Snow's recent but unfortunate incarceration. He will not be waiving his Fifth Amendment rights."

"Not a problem, your honor," Greenback said. "May I proceed?"

Johnson glared at Judge Stark as he said, "Yes, move it along."

Snow glanced at Tarina. He knew she would never understand why he'd worked with Zachary Cane to banish her. "Everything can be helped when it comes to family," she'd said at the jail. "You sided with Zachary Cane instead of your sister." But if he hadn't done it, he would not have earned Cane's confidence, and earning Cane's confidence had been the key to his long-term plan to save the North Pole from Cane.

"Mr. Snow, tell the court the name of your company."

"North Pole Enterprises."

"And what is its business?"

"We're an international toy company."

"Are you familiar with Tip Top Toy Company?"

Snow turned his head in the direction of the defense table, and looked past Raker and Sarah to where Tarina was sitting. "Yes, I am."

"What's its reputation?"

Snow had come to depend upon Tip Top Toy Company to do Santa's work. "It's a good company."

"What do you know about its owner, Tarina Winter?"

This is where Snow needed to get Raker riled up. He was counting on Raker to come after him during cross-examination. "She's a bit of a control freak."

"Objection," Raker said. "Lack of foundation."

"Overruled," Judge Johnson said. "Anyone who has been in this courtroom the last few days knows this man is telling the truth."

Greenback continued. "How long have you known Ms. Winter?"

"Many years."

"How would you describe your relationship with her?"

"I consider Tarina—" Snow stopped himself. "I consider Ms. Winter to be an important member of the toy-manufacturing community."

"Have you ever heard her talk about Santa Claus?"

"I have."

"Did you find that odd?"

"Not for her." He noticed Tarina's face tighten. It couldn't be helped.

"Did she speak of Santa often?"

"Whenever we had business together."

"And you were comfortable doing business with her?"

"Yes, she always delivered." This was true. Tarina had always come through for Santa Claus.

"So, you put up with her fantasy."

"Objection," Raker said.

"Overruled," Judge Johnson said. "Santa Claus is a fantasy."

"My question, Mr. Snow, is whether you put up with her belief in Santa Claus?"

"I'm not sure she did believe in him. She said he let her down." He knew Tarina would understand his word game. Greenback didn't because with his next question he used Snow's words to prove a point.

"Are you telling this court that Ms. Winter was so obsessed with Santa Claus that she thought him real enough to let her down?"

"I just know what she told me."

"Which was?"

"She told me she wondered why he didn't fight for her when she was banished."

"From where?" Judge Johnson asked.

"The North Pole." Half the audience erupted into laughter and Judge Johnson let them have their fun. Snow saw the anger in Raker's face. Good, he thought, he'll come after me.

"Do you think it's good for business for people to believe in Santa Claus?" Greenback asked.

"Not for my business." Snow was emphatic, satisfied with his own cleverness. The fewer believers in the world, the less it cost Santa to make Christmas possible.

"Why did you fund the study done by the League of Informed Entrepreneurs?"

"To document the harm caused by believing in Santa Claus." Snow didn't explain that after the

Henry Edmonds trial, Cane felt threatened by True Believers and he ordered Snow to do something about them. Snow knew it was a waste of time, that True Believers would win in the end, but he commissioned the 20-year study to buy time for him to try to gain control and oust Cane. Now Cane had the upper hand.

"Did Tip Top Toy Company design and manufacture the Reindeer Hoverboard?"

"Yes." This was a half-truth. Snow felt guilty that Tarina had taken all the blame.

"Have you examined the Reindeer Hoverboard?"

"I have."

"Is Santa Claus responsible for whether the Reindeer Hoverboard can fly?"

Snow wanted to make it sound as if he were undermining Tarina without telling a lie. His plan was coming together.

"Santa had nothing to do with it," Snow said.

Greenback smiled as if pleased with his own brilliance. "That's all we have for this witness, your honor." Greenback whispered to Tammy Brighthouse, who patted him on the shoulder. Judge Johnson ordered an early lunch break.

As Snow got up, he saw Raker pull several documents from an envelope. Snow recognized the envelope. It was the same one he'd had someone deliver to Austin Land. Good, he thought. Now things would get interesting.

Same Day – 1:30 p.m.

Snow returned to the witness chair and looked at Raker as the bailiff called the court to order. Raker leaned forward, the documents Snow had delivered to him at the ready and a notepad at their side. Judge Johnson told Raker to proceed.

"Mr. Snow, we meet again," Raker said.

"That we do."

"You seem to make it a practice to come to court and deny the existence of Santa Claus."

"It's a public place," Snow said. "That's as good a place as any to do so."

"Why?"

217

"You don't have to answer that, Mr. Snow," Judge Johnson said. He looked at Raker. "Telling the truth in court is not improper. Ask your next question."

"You're on LIE's board of directors, correct?"

"I am," Snow said.

"And you funded LIE's study, correct?"

"I did," Snow said.

"Isn't it fair to say that you align yourself with LIE?" Raker asked.

"We have some commons interests. For example, I agree with LIE's request that the court order Tip Top Toy Company not to deceive people about the existence of Santa Claus. Companies should not lie about things like that." He knew his continued denial of Santa's existence would irk Raker.

"Mr. Snow, please come down so we can examine the Reindeer Hoverboard."

The board lay on the floor in front of the judge's bench. When Snow got there, Raker said, "Please pick it up." Snow knew his refusal to do so would look suspicious, so he said, "No."

"What are you afraid of, Mr. Snow?"

"Nothing."

"Then stand on it. Surely, you can do that."

Snow was proud of Raker but grumbled to maintain the façade of noncooperation as he stepped on the hoverboard. The lights on the edges lit up and it began to hum. Raker took a step back and the audience and Judge Johnson stood to get a better view as the hoverboard rose in the air. Snow bent his knees like he was surfing a wave and the hoverboard tilted forward and started to move, slowly at first, and then it picked up speed. When it approached a side wall of the courtroom, Snow banked to the right and sailed past the head of a bailiff who backed out of the way. He shot down one side of the courtroom, banked 180 degrees and headed straight down the aisle in the direction of Judge Johnson, who had a startled look on his face.

When the hoverboard passed between the lawyers' desks at high speed, Snow jumped off. He landed on two feet in the middle of the courtroom just as the hoverboard hurtled at Judge Johnson's head. Johnson dove to the floor behind his bench. With a crash, the Reindeer Hoverboard slammed into the portrait of the late Honorable hanging on the wall and broke in two. One-half dropped to where Judge Johnson was hiding. The other half was lodged in the receding hairline of the deceased jurist.

Judge Johnson crawled out from under his bench and looked dazed. He brushed himself off and sat back down as Snow returned to the witness stand.

"Any further questions, Mr. Raker?" Judge Johnson said.

"Yes, sir," Raker said.

Raker pulled a document from his stack and took a close look at it. "You have experience designing things that fly, don't you?" he asked.

"I do."

"You developed drones to deliver Christmas presents for North Pole Enterprises, didn't you?"

"I did."

"What made them fly?"

At last, the right question. "A computer chip," Snow said.

Snow heard murmuring in the audience from both sides.

"Eight years ago, you became very concerned about the effects of global warming, didn't you?"

"True," Snow said. "That's one thing LIE and I don't agree on. I believe global warming is a threat to the environment."

"In response to that threat, you used your flying computer chip in another application, didn't you?"

"I did," Snow said, "but it didn't work."

"Please explain," Raker said.

"I used it to create a prototype for a drone evacuation program. Drones large enough to carry people."

"In case, for example," Raker said, "you needed to use it to evacuate anyone from the North Pole when the ice melts."

Laughter erupted from LIE's side of the courtroom. Snow was happy with the way things were going, but he needed to stay in character. "Mr. Raker, you have a vivid imagination. The prototype was for use in studying melting ice in remote locations. If a scientist got trapped while studying the ice, it could aid his escape."

"It didn't work, did it?" Raker asked.

"No," Snow admitted. "As you know, Mr. Raker, I haven't had much success with my inventions."

Raker asked and received permission to approach Snow and handed him a document to review.

"Do you recognize this document?" Raker asked.

Snow looked at it. He paused. He didn't want to appear to acknowledge the contents.

"Let me help you," Raker said. "This is a license agreement between North Pole Enterprises and Tip Top Toy Company, correct?"

Snow looked it over, hesitated and then said, "So."

"You gave Tip Top Toy Company the right to use your computer chip in the Reindeer Hoverboard, didn't you?"

"Yes, but the hoverboard was Tip Top Toy Company's idea." Snow played the part of being defensive.

"The point is," Raker said, "you, a self-identified, publicly declared nonbeliever, designed the chip. Based on that, instead of belief in Santa Claus determining whether or not the hoverboard flies, your poor design is to blame."

Snow squirmed and frowned, as if upset to have his design denigrated.

"Unless," Raker paused for effect, "you actually did design it to work only for people who believe in Santa Claus."

"I didn't do that," Snow said. "How could I? There's no such person as Santa Claus." Snow thought this was working out well. Now Raker just needed to finish him off.

"Tell the court about the warning," Raker said. "It was your idea, wasn't it?"

"I thought it would help sell hoverboards around Christmas."

"That's because you stood to profit, right?"

"Sure," Snow said, "I'm a businessman."

"Isn't it true, your contract with Tip Top Toy Company required that all proceeds for the first year's sales go directly to North Pole Enterprises?"

Snow nodded.

"Is that a 'yes' for the record?"

"Yes," Snow said, as if he had something to hide.

"So, let me get this straight," Raker said. "You designed a computer chip that is faulty. You came up with a marketing idea to get people to buy the hoverboard at Christmas and, as we speak, every bit of the money plaintiffs paid for the product is in a North Pole Enterprises bank account. Tip Top Toy Company didn't deceive or take the plaintiffs' money. You did."

"It's not my problem, Mr. Raker."

"True," Raker said. "The problem is, the plaintiffs sued the wrong company. They should have sued North Pole Enterprises."

Snow knew Raker had done as much as he could. "You know, Mr. Raker," Snow said. "You are exactly right, but I could not care less. I've got a little problem of my own in federal court."

"That's all the questions I have, your honor." Raker sat down.

Snow looked at Judge Johnson, who appeared unsure as to how to proceed. Finally, he said to the lawyers, "Any more witnesses?" They all said no, and he ordered a 30-minute break, "to prepare my ruling."

Snow looked at Greenback and Brighthouse, who were huddled in conversation. It was time for Step 2 of his plan.

Settlement in Progress

Same Day – 2:30 p.m.

Judge Stark was happy with his client. Hank Snow's performance had been a tour de force. He smiled as he approached Greenback and Brighthouse. "I think we should talk."

"About what?" Greenback asked.

"Just have your clients in the anteroom in five minutes. I promise you it will be worth their time." He didn't wait for them to respond. His next visit was with one of the bailiffs, who was seated next to Hank Snow, guarding him.

"Hello, Ralph. How have you and your lovely wife been doing?"

"Fine, your honor." The bailiff was on his feet. "We miss having you around here to keep order."

"Miss my rules of court, do you?"

"Yes, sir, you ran a tight ship, if you don't mind me saying so."

"Not at all." Judge Stark motioned for him to sit and then took a seat beside him. "Ralph, I think I may have a way to resolve this case and avoid an appeal of Judge Johnson's decision. If he gets reversed on appeal, he'll make your lives miserable."

"What can I do to help, sir?" Ralph asked.

"I need to borrow my client for about 10 minutes. Conference in the anteroom. I'll bring him back."

Ralph said, "But—"

"I know. You're worried about what Judge Johnson will say. I promise I'll have him back before court resumes. You can stand outside the anteroom if it will make you feel better. It's not like he's going to fly off."

Ralph let out a nervous laugh. "Okay, but hurry it up. I don't want to lose my job."

"Good man," Judge Stark said. He reached over and tugged on Snow's coat. "Let's go."

When they arrived at the anteroom, Greenback and Brighthouse were there with their clients, Martin Stubble and Dr. Wingnut.

"What's this all about?" Brighthouse said. "Judge Johnson is going to rule for plaintiffs, so this better be good."

"She's right," Greenback said. "Our clients are in the driver's seat. Tip Top Toy Company is about to be roadkill, and we can go after your client, too."

"This is about settlement," Judge Stark said. "Your clients came to court to get something of value. Judge Johnson may rule in your favor, but appeals can be a hassle and enforcing a judgment against a company headquartered in Greenland will be tricky. Especially since that company doesn't even have your money. If you file suit against my client, that will take more money and more time. It may be years before the plaintiffs see a penny."

"What's the offer?" Stubble asked.

"One question," Judge Stark said to Stubble. "Where are the hoverboards?"

"I collected a large supply from plaintiffs so we could return them if the court ordered Tip Top Toy Company to refund our money. They're stored in a warehouse near my hometown in Maine."

"How many have you collected?" Snow asked.

"About 10,000 so far."

Judge Stark looked at Snow, who said, "That should work."

Judge Stark focused on Stubble again. "If you can get the plaintiffs a great deal, can you sell it to them?"

"Sure, if it's a great deal, I can sell it."

"What about us?" Dr. Wingnut asked. "The League of Informed Entrepreneurs needs to be satisfied, too."

"You're the easy part," Judge Stark said. "The settlement offer will address all your concerns."

"So," Brighthouse said, "what's the offer?"

"Before Hank Snow explains the terms, you each need to understand his ability to deliver on his promises." Judge Stark turned to Snow. "Please tell Mr. Greenback what he received for Christmas as an 8-year-old boy."

Snow smiled. "A skateboard."

"Please tell Ms. Brighthouse what she received for Christmas as an 8-year-old girl."

Snow laughed. "Coal."

"Mr. Stubble?"

"A kite," Snow said, "and a rocket set. He always loved toys that fly."

"Dr. Wingnut?"

"Books. Mostly about fantasy."

Greenback leaned back in his chair. "What kind of tricks are you people playing? First Mr. Snow flies around the courtroom on a hoverboard that's not supposed to fly, and now he's guessing what we got for Christmas as children."

"He's not guessing," Judge Stark said. "Ask him anything you want about your Christmas experiences as children."

For the next five minutes, the lawyers and their clients peppered Snow with questions. Their faces showed more confusion with every answer they received.

"How could anyone know the answers to these questions?" Stubble asked.

"Not just anyone could," Judge Stark said. "Only someone who works for Santa Claus can."

Brighthouse was on her feet. "That's preposterous."

"Do you have a better explanation?" Judge Stark asked.

"But he admitted in court that Santa's not real," Brighthouse said.

"And he funded LIE's study," Wingnut added.

"You're both right," Judge Stark said. "Fact is, you should be happy. In public, he will support your proselytizing that Santa is nothing but fantasy."

For a full minute, no one spoke. Judge Stark looked at his watch. There were 10 minutes left until Judge Johnson wanted everyone back in court.

"Time for you to make your best offer," Judge Stark said to Snow.

Snow got right to work and made his pitch. After he finished, Judge Stark knew Snow had made the sale.

"Time to get back to court," Judge Stark said to Stubble and Wingnut. "Your lawyers can let the judge know if we have a deal."

Raker was seated with Sarah and Tarina when he saw Judge Stark and Hank Snow return to the courtroom, followed closely by Greenback, Brighthouse and their clients. He wondered if they'd been together and, if so, what they'd talked about.

Before Raker could ask Judge Stark where he'd been, the side door opened and Judge Johnson returned. He had a spring in his step.

"Good, good," Judge Johnson said. "Everyone is here. Take your seats, so you can hear my ruling."

"Your honor," Judge Stark said, "may I—"

"No, you may not," Johnson said. "Sit down."

Johnson had some papers in his hands, which he tamped on the bench to line them up. He smiled at everyone in the courtroom and then started to read. Raker's heart sank as he listened to the words. The court was denying the jury trial, striking the defense, entering an injunction prohibiting lies about the existence of Santa Claus, awarding compensatory and punitive damages and throwing in attorney fees and costs for good measure. Tip Top Toy Company had lost in every possible way. It would mean bankruptcy for the company, and no safe haven for the Santa Relocation Plan.

Raker felt awful. He'd let his client down. The worst part was that of all the Christmas trials he'd ever handled, this one mattered most, and he'd lost.

"Mr. Greenback, Ms. Brighthouse, draw up the judgment and I will sign it," Judge Johnson said.

Raker expected the gloating to begin, but the opposing lawyers looked at each other and didn't respond.

"Is there a problem?" Judge Johnson asked.

"I think what they're going to tell you," Judge Stark said, "is, there is no need for the judgment."

"What are you talking about?" Judge Johnson didn't look happy. His former nemesis was undermining his grand ruling. Raker felt the tide might be turning ever so slightly in his favor, though he didn't understand how.

Greenback and Brighthouse stood up. "It's true," Greenback said, "the parties have reached a settlement, subject to the court's approval." Brighthouse concurred.

Judge Johnson looked at Raker. "Is that true?"

No one had told him anything about a settlement, but whatever it was had to be better than Judge Johnson's version of justice. "Your honor, I'm probably not the best person to explain the settlement."

"What is it you want the court to approve, Mr. Greenback?"

"Each of the plaintiffs in the class will receive five times the value of their hoverboards."

"Paid when and by whom?" Judge Johnson asked.

Greenback looked uneasy. "These are in-kind gifts from North Pole Enterprises. They are due in installments over the next five years."

Snow leaned over and whispered to Judge Stark.

"Excuse me, your honor." Judge Stark was on his feet. "There is one condition to the annual compensation—or gifts shall we say—that are due on Christmas Day of each year."

"Is that right, Greenback?" Judge Johnson's voice showed his patience was wearing thin.

Again, Greenback looked uncomfortable with the question. "Yes, sir, there is a condition."

"What is it?"

"My clients have to be Nice."

"Excuse me?" Judge Johnson looked perplexed.

"Look at it this way, your honor," Judge Stark said. "You will turn some litigious people into upstanding citizens."

"And what do I get to do to Tip Top Toy Company?" Judge Johnson asked.

"Off the hook, financially," Judge Stark said. Raker looked at Tarina and saw relief written on her face. Sarah touched his arm and he knew she was hopeful.

"But with one condition," Brighthouse added. "They can't promote the existence of Santa Claus."

"Is that right, Raker?" Judge Johnson didn't seem to like the settlement. Perhaps he hoped Raker would object.

"If I may have a moment with my client, your honor." Raker leaned over and whispered to Tarina. "This is better than the alternative."

"Ask about the hoverboards," she whispered. "We need to get them back."

Raker stood. "Your honor, my client would appreciate plaintiffs clarifying for the record the settlement terms regarding the hoverboards."

Greenback offered to address the point. "Over the next three months, the hoverboards will be returned, but 10,000 of them are available now to be picked up by North Pole Enterprises or Tip Top Toy Company."

Tarina flashed the first smile Raker had seen from her since the day she was held in contempt of court. "Tell the judge we agree."

Raker wasn't sure why the return of the hoverboards was important to Tarina, but he didn't wait to ask. "Tip Top Toy Company agrees to the settlement."

Judge Johnson looked disappointed. "This is what everyone wants?" Everyone said they did. He still looked hesitant. "Don't we need to have a fairness hearing, so any class members can object?"

"The settlement offer is contingent on the settlement being approved today," Judge Stark said.

"What about it, Greenback?" Judge Johnson asked.

Greenback huddled with Martin Stubble and then had his answer. "Mr. Stubble has the authority to settle on behalf of the class for at least three times what they paid for the hoverboards. This settlement is within his authority."

"Fine," Judge Johnson said. "The class action settlement is approved. Now get out of my courtroom. All of you." He slammed his gavel on the bench and its head came off.

Thursday, December 20th

Raker was on his way to Judge Stark's house in the hope that Judge Stark would shed some light on Snow's behavior. After the trial, he and Sarah had discussed how out of character it had been for Snow to save Tip Top Toy Company and Raker was searching for answers.

As he turned onto the street where Judge Stark lived, he felt guilty about the way he had judged Snow. He knew why he'd done it. Snow had opposed him in the Henry Edmonds and the Twirly Masters trials. It seemed only logical that Snow was against him, again, in the Tip Top Toy Company case. Yesterday in court made Raker wonder if Snow had changed.

Raker was surprised to see swirling red lights on the roof of an ambulance parked in Judge Stark's driveway. He stopped his car, jumped out and ran to the ambulance. A medic was about to close the back doors when Raker grabbed his arm. "Who's in there?"

"Old man. Hurt bad. Got to get him to the hospital."

Raker looked inside. "I'm going with you."

"I can't allow that," the medic said.

"We're related," Raker lied. He climbed in before the medic could object again.

When the back doors slammed shut, Raker crouched on one side of the stretcher that held the prone body of Judge Augustus Langhorne Stark. A medic was on the other side, monitoring the judge's vitals. His eyes were shut. His breathing shallow. By the look of the swelling in his midsection, he'd suffered severe trauma to his torso.

"What happened?" Raker asked the medic.

"The mailman found him in the side yard 30 minutes ago, with this strange surfboard thing lying beside him. By his condition, I'd say he had a severe fall and he's been there a while."

Raker placed his hand on the judge's forehead and rubbed his arm. "Hang in there, Judge. We're going to get you some help." Judge Stark didn't respond.

"Is he going to be okay?" Raker asked the medic.

"It doesn't look good. He probably has internal bleeding. Probably damaged some organs. How are you related?"

Raker struggled to answer. His parents died when he was young and until he met Judge Stark, he'd never had a mentor. Over the years, Judge Stark had been hard on him in court, but Raker came to realize it was because he cared. He wanted Raker to succeed. Out of court, Judge Stark had become a perfect grandfather to Liz. Raker wiped his eye, to catch a tear.

Before Raker could explain his relationship to Judge Stark, the ambulance hit a pothole that caused the head of the stretcher to bounce a foot off the floor. When the stretcher came down, Judge Stark's head banged on its metal rim, causing him to grimace, forcing his eyes to open.

"Judge Stark, can you hear me?"

Judge Stark turned his head toward Raker's voice. "Thad, what's going on here?" His voice was weak.

"You've had an accident."

"Dang hoverboard. I was just getting the hang of it when an owl swooped across my bow and made me lose my balance." He looked around. "Ambulance?"

"Yes, we're taking you to the hospital."

"How bad is it?" Judge Stark grimaced again and reached for his midsection. "Don't sugarcoat it. Remember my rules. Credibility is most important."

Raker looked at the medic, who said, "Sir, you've suffered a serious blow to your midsection. You may have damaged vital organs. Your blood pressure is fading."

Judge Stark was quiet for a moment and then he started to laugh, only to grab his midsection and gasp for breath. "Never thought this would be the way I'd go, Thad, but you have to admit, it's better than tripping on a walker or banging my head on a bedpan in some nursing home."

"Yes, sir," Raker said.

Over the next five minutes, between short spasms when the judge tried to catch his breath, he reminisced. He talked about the things he loved. Growing up on a farm. The first wild trout he caught. Being the first in his family to go to law school. Forever grateful for the scholarship he received. His wife, Kay, the one true love in his life. He looked forward to seeing her again. And finally, his career as a lawyer and judge. Where he met good lawyers like Thad Raker and Sarah Kennedy. Always loved the law. Loved them, too. Hoped he'd made a difference in the law and in their lives.

Raker and the medic didn't interrupt. The blood pressure monitor did. It beeped. Not much time left.

Judge Stark reached up with his right hand. Raker placed his two hands around it and bent over.

"Thad, things are not always as they seem. People can change, make amends for their prior misdeeds."

Was he talking about Hank Snow? Raker wondered.

The judge looked weaker but appeared determined to be heard. "I want you to do something for me. Promise me." He was fading. Raker waited for him to continue.

"Represent Hank Snow. Defend him as you've never defended a client in a Christmas trial before. He is the key to the future of Christmas."

Raker didn't understand. How could Hank Snow be the future of Christmas?

"Promise me, Thad?"

He nodded. "I promise."

Judge Stark lay his head back on the pillow, mumbling. Raker leaned in to listen. "Tell Liz I love her, not to take this hard—it's my time—and tell her—" He struggled to get out his last words. "Tell her to always believe."

Raker couldn't hear the sounds around him. Not the siren. Not the honking of horns. Not the beeping of the blood-pressure monitor. Not the efforts of the medic to revive the judge. All he heard was the last breath of the greatest judge and friend he'd ever known.

The medic pulled the sheet up to cover the smile that was emblematic of a remarkable life. He tugged it a little farther to cover Judge Stark's entire head. Raker buried his own in his hands and wept.

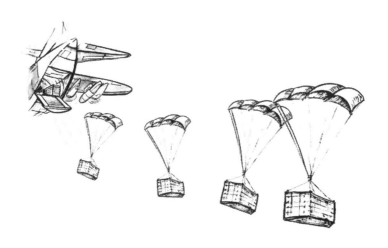

Friday, December 21ˢᵗ

Liz sensed that their time at Santa's village was running out. Snowflake, Holly and she had just downloaded all the data from the village computers onto thumb-sized hard drives and packed them, along with books, manuals and historical records, in their knapsacks.

"When—not if—we escape," Snowflake said, "we will preserve the history of the North Pole, including all the records of Christmas past. We're also going to take as much operational information as we can carry for use at Santa's new home."

"Nothing on these drives or in these books is going to be nearly as interesting as the last few months," Holly said.

"Or the next 24 hours," Liz added.

Snowflake laughed. "Just keep working."

Liz knew Snowflake was trying to keep their minds focused on the tasks at hand and off of what was coming. In the last 12 hours, the creaking and moaning of the ice sheet had gotten louder and more frequent, and the basement at The Archives was full of water. It was just a matter of time. If they stayed here, they wouldn't live to see Christmas.

"What are our chances?" Liz asked Snowflake.

Snowflake stopped packing and gave them her full attention. "I believe our chances are good. Hank Snow is determined to save us."

"How do you know?" Holly asked.

"After Hank Snow emailed the document he found at the White House, he mailed the original to me." Snowflake pulled the document out of her knapsack and held it up for the girls to see. "He attached this note to the document. It says, 'Activate the SRP. I'm going to evacuate everyone before Christmas.'"

"Can we trust him?" Liz asked.

"I do," Snowflake said. "The elves do, too."

"But even if we escape," Liz said, "what about Christmas? We can't move the presents."

Holly had the answer. "As part of the Santa Relocation Plan, the elves loaded this year's Christmas presents onto ships bound for northern Greenland before the lockdown went into effect. The presents left the village just in time. Twirly Masters will oversee their intake for distribution on Christmas Eve."

"That's great," Liz said, "but what about everything else? The equipment? The supplies?"

"Not as important as the gifts, the historical records and the elf community," Snowflake said. "The gifts for this Christmas will be safe. We'll take the historical records with us when everyone leaves."

Their conversation was interrupted by voices outside the door. Someone spoke with their guards, but the person's words could not be understood. One of the guards said in a loud response, "Mrs. Claus is confined to quarters, by order of Chairman Cane."

The first speaker laughed, a deep laugh that echoed in the crisp night air. "That's what you think. Now out of our way before I put you on the Naughty list."

The door banged open and snow swirled around two figures silhouetted against the night sky. "Ho, ho, ho, and Merry Christmas," one of them said. "Just four days until Christmas. Exciting, don't you think?" It was the head elf himself: Santa Claus.

Mrs. Claus pushed him into the room and shut the door behind them. "He's nothing but a kid at Christmastime," she said. "Hard to get him to focus on the danger we face."

"Hello, Santa," Snowflake said. "Welcome to The Archives. You know Holly. Permit me to introduce Liz Raker."

"Hello, Liz," Santa said. "My, my. You have been a good girl this year. Stirring up trouble but definitely of the Nice variety. Thank you for all you've done."

Liz was speechless. She was a True Believer, but believing is one thing. Seeing is something entirely different. Like Mrs. Claus, Santa didn't fit the image she had in her mind. He was big but fit. A strong man. She supposed that made sense, given the life he'd lived and the work he performed, but it was startling to see how vigorous he was. He wore black wool pants and a white flight jacket with red trim. Even his beard was not as she expected. Salty gray and neatly trimmed. But the rosy cheeks betrayed him, definitely the Santa she imagined, and he had a killer smile.

"The boy has a good plan." Santa turned his head to listen. "Do you hear that?" he asked.

Everyone became quiet, attentive. Liz didn't hear anything. She listened harder and then she heard the sound of an engine in the night sky. She ran to the window to look out and everyone crowded around her to see. A long line of bright white parachutes with fluorescent trim trailed out of the back of a cargo plane that flew over the ice sheet at a low altitude.

"He did it," Santa said.

A loud bang interrupted him. It came from just below their feet and was followed by the floor splitting apart, dividing Santa and Mrs. Claus on one side from everyone else on the other. The crack became larger.

Mrs. Claus said, "Oh, no. It's happening."

Santa laughed so hard his belly shook, which had the effect of calming everyone in the room. When he had their attention, he said, "Snowflake, sound the alarm. I will hook the reindeer to the sleigh. Mrs. Claus and I will bring up the rear once I know everyone is safely off the ice sheet."

"But how?" Liz asked.

"Hoverboards," Santa said. "Or, I should say, Reindeer Hoverboards."

Saturday, December 22nd

Snow was in an empty interview room at the county jail, hands and feet shackled. His jailer had just informed him that his lawyer had died in an accident. That was a shock. He liked Judge Stark. The judge was practical, like Snow, and had a sharp mind. Snow couldn't have navigated the Tip Top Toy Company case without him.

The door opened and three people walked in. Tarina Winter was flanked by Thad Raker on one side and Sarah Kennedy on the other. "I've brought you a new legal team," she said.

"Judge Stark's idea," Raker added.

247

"Why would you want to represent me?" Snow asked.

"We both want to represent you," Sarah said. "We trust Judge Stark. He said you are the future of Christmas."

Snow wasn't sure. Though he'd helped Tarina with her lawsuit, he'd made too many mistakes to be a leader. He'd underestimated Cane, botched the Edmonds and Masters trials, gotten arrested for breaking into the White House and all of his technological inventions had failed. He changed the subject. "I'm sorry to hear about Judge Stark."

Before anyone could respond, the phone in Raker's pocket rang. He answered it, listened and said, "That's great news." He hung up and looked at Snow.

"What was that about?" Snow asked.

"You finally invented something that works," Raker said. "The Reindeer Hoverboard saved everyone at the North Pole."

He turned to Sarah. "Liz is safe. She's in northern Greenland. She should be home tomorrow afternoon."

"That's great news." Sarah hugged him.

Tarina agreed. "Way to go, little brother." She patted him on the shoulder.

"Judge Stark would be proud of you," Sarah said to Snow.

"I'm very grateful, too," Raker said.

"Okay, that's enough," Tarina said, "If Judge Stark were here, he'd tell us to stop socializing and get to work. Hank is facing a long prison sentence and his court date is on Christmas Eve. We have to figure a way to set him free. Santa and the elves need him. Christmas needs him."

Snow appreciated the support but was reluctant to accept the help. He didn't want to go to jail, but having a trial could mean revealing too many truths. "I'd rather not have a public trial," Snow said. "Too many secrets that need to stay that way."

"What is the truth about you?" Raker asked. "I've been wondering about that for a long time."

Tarina spoke first. "Just before we came in," she said to Snow, "I explained to Thad and Sarah that you're my half-brother. You should tell them the rest of our family secret and then listen to their advice."

Snow decided it was time. "I suppose you deserve to know the truth," he said. "After Tarina's father died, her mother married Santa Claus. They had one child. Me."

Raker's mouth fell open and Sarah covered hers with her hands.

"That's right," Snow said. "If Dad falls out of the sleigh or gets run over by a reindeer, you're looking at the new Santa. How do you think the Christmas Eve suit will fit a frame like this?" Snow tried to make an outward motion with his arms but the handcuffs kept his arms tight to his body.

"But why didn't you tell us you were Santa's son?" Sarah asked.

"Very few people know. My parents. Tarina. The midwife. Possibly, Snowflake. And now the two of you."

"I don't understand," Raker said. "Why would your parents keep this a secret?"

"Two words," Snow said. "Zachary Cane. If he had known I was Santa's heir, he would have figured a way to banish me, even as a child. When I was only 25 years old, Cane locked horns with Tarina, who was trying to make life better for the elves. My parents wanted to tell him the truth about me to take the pressure off of her, but I said no. I didn't want Cane to have any clue what he was up against."

"Hank supported Cane's desire to banish me and made it happen," Tarina said. "I didn't know why at the time, and I hated him for it." She touched Snow on the shoulder. "Now I know he did it for the greater good of the North Pole, and that's why Santa didn't interfere with his plan."

"The only way to beat Cane was to get close to him," Snow explained. "Earn his confidence. I did all the dirty work, including what he wanted done in the Edmonds and Masters trials."

"What went wrong with your plan?" Raker asked.

"My arrest," Snow said.

"Perhaps if you tell us what happened," Sarah said, "we can figure out a way to help you keep Santa's secrets and still not go to prison."

Snow figured it couldn't hurt. "In recent years, the worldwide Christmas grid has experienced security problems. We had a near-miss last year when Santa was delivering presents at the Vatican in the Italian zone. He landed fine, but when he entered down the stack at the Sistine Chapel—the one where the smoke drifts out during a papal conclave—an alarm went off. They almost nabbed Santa as an intruder."

"It's true," Tarina said. "We were about to activate backup Santa."

Snow saw the lawyers' perplexed looks but didn't stop to explain. "The same thing happened at the

251

Quirinal Palace of the Italian president and other state residences in other countries," Snow said. "We needed to know how to avoid triggering alarms. If we couldn't, we'd have to stop deliveries to our strongest allies."

"Hold on," Raker said. "You're telling us that the heads of state around the world are True Believers?"

"Of course," Tarina said. "When the economy is suffering, there's no better way to take the voters' minds off of unfulfilled campaign promises than Christmas. Santa has always been a politician's best friend."

Sarah laughed. "You mean to tell me that the president of the United States is a True Believer? I never would have guessed."

"He is," Snow said, "but he's on the Naughty list this year after the document I found at the White House."

"Tell us about the document," Raker said.

Snow explained the deal that was struck between the U.S. president, the premier of the People's Republic of China and the Russian president to sacrifice the environment and split the mineral rights to the North Pole. "The business deal was a new form of détente," Snow said. "They even concealed the deal from their allies."

Sarah had a question. "How did your discovery of this document cause Cane to turn on you?" she asked.

"Cane wanted to use it to blackmail the three governments. He said he would cut me in on the profits. I refused because I wanted to protect the North Pole, but I was in jail and couldn't do anything. Tarina told me he circulated a story at the North Pole about me being the traitor. He knew I wouldn't turn over the document to free myself. I was stuck then. I'm stuck now."

Raker stopped making notes on his legal pad. "What would be so wrong with more people knowing for sure that Santa Claus is real and learning the truth about you?"

"It's my philosophy," Snow said, "that believing without seeing is the real magic in this world. It's the kind of magic that's really worth preserving."

"That's a wonderful sentiment," Sarah said.

"I never thought I would agree with you about anything," Raker said to Snow, "but I agree with you now. You're exactly right."

Snow grinned. "So now that we're best friends, who has an idea for how to get me out of here without disclosing Santa's secrets to the public? I'd like to get to work at my new home in Greenland."

"How good are you at bluffing?" Raker asked.

"Been doing it all my life," Snow said.

When Raker explained what he had in mind, Snow smiled. "It just might work."

Sunday, December 23rd

Liz landed at her hometown airport and went through customs. Nothing to declare, she told the agent. She carried only her knapsack of books and paperwork.

As she walked the long hallway to the passenger collection area, she thought about the last few months. Meeting Tarina. Touring Tip Top Toy Company. Convening the Band of True Believers. Inspecting the underground village. The midnight sleigh ride to the North Pole. Facing down Cane. Meeting Santa and Mrs. Claus. The fantastic hoverboard ride across the Arctic Ocean, stopping from time to time to rest on icebergs. It was going to be hard to top this adventure.

She also thought about her departure from Greenland. It was hard to say goodbye to Snowflake, Holly, Mistletoe, Henry and Twirly. They remained behind to get everything set up at Santa's new village and to assist with Christmas deliveries. To pull this Christmas off, Santa needed all the help he could get. She wanted to stay, too, but as Snowflake told her, she had a mission.

When she'd boarded the plane, she called her dad. It was great to hear his voice, but there was something in it that was off, like he was holding something back. She pressed him, reminding him of their agreement not to keep secrets from each other. That was when he told her the news that Judge Stark had passed on.

On the flight home, Liz had cried most of the way. She wiped at her eyes one last time. She was here to help her dad fulfill Judge Stark's last request.

When she left the terminal, she saw Sarah. They ran to each other and hugged. "Your dad is parked over there." Sarah pointed.

Two minutes later, Liz was in her father's arms. "I've missed you, Liz. We were worried about you. But I'm proud of you. So very proud."

"Thanks, Daddy." She pulled back and said, "But there's more work to be done."

"Right," he said. "Do you have the document?"

She unlatched her knapsack and handed the envelope to Raker. He opened it and slid the paper out. Glancing over it, he said, "It's hard to believe that the heads of state of the three most powerful governments in the world believe in Santa Claus."

Monday, December 24th

Raker and Sarah sat at the defense counsel table in the federal courtroom and waited for the U.S. marshal to bring Hank Snow into the room.

"It's a full house," Raker said.

"They want to see the man who could break into the White House and almost get away with it," Sarah said. "I see FBI Agent Lemming over there. And I recognize the head of the National Security Council next to the U.S. attorney."

"I guess this is another trial of the century for us," Raker said. She smiled.

The bailiff rose and called the courtroom to order. Federal Judge J. P. Lake entered and took her seat. Everyone sat and came to order. "Mr. Raker and Ms. Kennedy, I understand you have substituted in as defense counsel in place of Judge Stark and that he was a friend of yours. I'm sorry for your loss. He was a great judge."

"Thank you," they said. Raker knew that Judge Lake had been close to Judge Stark. He wondered whether that would help.

The side door opened and Hank Snow was brought into the courtroom, dressed in a suit. No handcuffs. The U.S. marshal walked him over to Raker and Sarah and he took a seat next to them. Raker patted him on the shoulder.

Judge Lake looked at the U.S. attorney and asked, "Are you ready to proceed?"

"Yes, your honor."

Raker stood up. "Your honor, my client waives reading of the charges."

"He's ready to plead?" she asked.

"Yes," Raker said, "and he'd like to make a statement—about a certain document."

The man Sarah had recognized next to the U.S. attorney stood up. "Your honor, Cecil Melvin, chairman of the National Security Council. We have a motion for the court to consider, to bar any discussion of the document in open court. May we approach?"

Raker leaned over and whispered to Snow. "Remind you of anything? Man involved in security interrupts a trial, seeking to prevent the disclosure of confidential information. Exactly what you did at the Henry Edmonds trial."

Judge Lake took the motion papers, read the first page and then scanned the rest quickly. She took off her reading glasses and said, "Ladies and gentlemen, we need to clear the courtroom for me to take up this matter."

This set the courtroom abuzz. Reporters scratched on notepads or tapped on computers. This was the stir Raker wanted. He looked to Sarah and smiled. She smiled back.

When the courtroom was empty of all spectators, Judge Lake asked Mr. Melvin why he didn't want Mr. Snow to talk about the document he'd allegedly stolen from the White House.

"It's a matter of national security," he said.

Judge Lake didn't hesitate. "Mr. Melvin, you're in my courtroom now. You're not on Capitol Hill. If you want me to consider your motion, I have to know more."

"Excuse me, your honor," Melvin said. He conferred with the U.S. attorney, who nodded, and offered a proposal. "If defendant returns the document and agrees to plead guilty to the lesser offense of breaking and entering, the government will drop the charge of treasonous theft and recommend a five-year sentence for the lesser charge."

"What do you say to that, Mr. Raker?" Judge Lake asked.

Raker had anticipated this move. "Not interested, your honor. My client would prefer to plead guilty to all charges."

"Why would he do that?"

"He's prepared to serve his time so that the contents of the document can be made public. He'll feel good knowing he's done the right thing."

This set off whispering among the U.S. attorney, his staff, Agent Lemming and the chairman of the National Security Council. Raker noticed that Judge Lake had a thin smile on her face. Hank Snow leaned over to Raker and whispered, "Did you know that Judge Lake is a True Believer?"

"I knew I liked her," Raker said.

Melvin pushed the U.S. attorney forward to say, "We object, your honor."

"I'm sorry," Judge Lake said. "Did you say you object to the defendant pleading guilty to the charges you have brought against him?"

The U.S. attorney looked around for help from Melvin.

"Your honor," Melvin said, "his threat to release the contents of the document is itself a criminal offense."

"What do you want to do?"

"With the court's permission," Melvin said, "we would like to have 20 minutes to discuss a plea deal with the defendant and his attorneys."

"Seems like they took your bait," Snow whispered to Raker.

"Your honor," Raker said, "we will be glad to speak with Chairman Melvin, the U.S. attorney and the FBI, provided they invite the Russian and Chinese ambassadors to the meeting. They're waiting outside."

Snow sat next to his lawyers at a long table in a conference room with a high ceiling and gray walls. The U.S. attorney, Cecil Melvin, Agent Lemming and the Russian and Chinese ambassadors sat on the other side of the table.

Melvin was the first to speak, "You've had your fun, Raker. If your client doesn't release the document to us, we will make his life miserable."

"By 'we,' do you mean the three co-conspirators: the United States government, the Russian government and the Chinese government?"

"We can charge you and your wife, too," Melvin said. "Strip you of your law licenses. End your careers. Keep you separate and apart, and in prison for a long, long time."

Snow felt his blood pressure rise. "I was going to let my lawyers handle this, but I don't like the way you're trying to intimidate them. This will be more efficient if you hear it from me."

Melvin smiled. "Good, because you're the reason we're here. You need to—"

Snow interrupted. "Let me tell you how this is going to work. Each of you is going to listen to what I have to say and then you can decide whether you want to do business with me or suffer the consequences."

"This sounds like blackmail," Melvin said. "We can just add that to the list of charges."

"I don't care what you call it," Snow said. "Blackmail, political compromise, plea bargain, business deal, whatever. The point is, if you want to hear the deal, you shut up and listen." That caught their attention.

"The document you want to keep secret is the most corrupt business deal between foreign governments in history. I understand the motivation. Twenty percent of the world's supply of oil and natural gas lies below the Arctic Ocean, along with substantial untapped minerals that can drive your industrialized economies. Phosphate, bauxite, iron ore, copper and nickel. But conspiring to sacrifice the environment to steal those minerals is unforgivable. That's why you're going to do some things you don't want to do."

"Like what?" Melvin asked.

"The U.S. Attorney's office will dismiss the case against me and I will walk out of here a free man."

"We can't do that," the U.S. attorney said. "How will we explain to the public dismissing charges against a man who broke into the White House?"

"You'll think of something," Snow said. "Next, you're all familiar with the Paris Agreement. Your countries signed the accord to reduce the impact of greenhouse gas emissions on the world's environment and you've been acting like it never happened. But here's the good news. You're going to do better than the Paris Agreement and you're going to lead by example. Your three countries are going to sign the most progressive accord in history designed to control global warming, and you will encourage other countries to join you."

Melvin said, "The political climate is not right."

The ambassadors nodded and murmured agreement, but Snow saw the Chinese ambassador wipe his brow and the Russian ambassador begin to study the ceiling. He imagined them contemplating what they would tell their leaders about how they botched the negotiation, and what might happen to them after they were relieved of their duties.

"Well, here's a little truth for you to consider," Snow said. "For decades, the three most powerful governments in the world have known with certainty that global warming is reality and have conspired to make it worse. If you don't play by these rules, we will expose the truth to the world."

"Anything else?" Melvin asked.

"Yes. Three more things," Snow said. "First, if Zachary Cane contacts you, you will not pay him one single dollar, ruble or renminbi. Second, the North Pole ice sheet is in pieces, thanks to you. As a result, you will use your votes and influence at the United Nations to preserve the North Pole area as international waters. Global warming has set the stage for more sea travel and mining. You will ensure that the use of the area is shared by all."

"What's the last thing?" Melvin asked.

"You will like this," Snow said. "You will not tell the world that Santa Claus is real. We can admit it in here. But out there," Snow pointed to the door. "Out there, people have to become True Believers in their hearts, based on their own beliefs. No documents. No pictures. Nothing. Or else—"

"Or else what?" Melvin asked.

"Have you ever heard of SantaLeaks?" Snow asked.

"No."

"Kind of like WikiLeaks but with a heart. It's run by a friend of mine, an elf named Snowflake. We've never had to use it, but it's set up and ready to go. If you violate your end of the deal, your precious document gets released to the entire world. Keep in mind, we have a pretty big mailing list."

"Wait," Melvin said, "you're going to keep a copy of the document?"

"Two to be exact," Snow said. "One will be with SantaLeaks and the other will be in a place only known to a few select people."

"But how can we trust you?"

Raker responded. "Hank Snow does not want Santa's reality to be revealed to the world. Check out the transcripts of his testimony in three trials in this county where he denied Santa's existence. I can assure you he will reveal the document only if he must, to keep you honest."

"You get the original," Snow said. "The copies are our leverage, because I know your past, Mr. Melvin. You were on the Naughty list more than once growing up and your bad habits haven't changed much since then."

"What about Zachary Cane? How will you prevent him from releasing the document if we don't pay him?"

"The keeper of the North Pole Archives wiped his computers, deleted his email accounts and located and destroyed the copy he printed and hid. His bargaining power is as thin as the broken ice he has left behind."

Melvin huddled with the two ambassadors. Snow gave them 30 seconds, and then interrupted. "Do we have a deal?"

"We need a few more minutes," Melvin said.

"Look at it this way," Snow said. "By doing your part to address global warming, you can save Christmas for your great-grandchildren. Your misconduct destroyed Santa's village and made refugees of the elf population that served the world for centuries, but we have a new home, at another frozen tundra. Take the right environmental steps and you'll keep Santa in business for a long, long time."

Snow looked at his watch. "We have three minutes before we have to be back in court."

"What about the original?" Melvin asked.

"When you tell the judge you want to dismiss the charges against me, someone will hand the original document to Agent Lemming."

Snow put his hands on the table, leaned forward and spoke truth to power. "But if any of you go back on your word, SantaLeaks will release the document and set you straight. It will be the biggest lump of coal Santa ever had to deliver."

Judge Lake was in her seat and ready to proceed. The spectators were back. An overflow audience was on hand and people crowded in to stand in the back. Word must have gotten out about the national security issue and the plea conference because more reporters had shown up and there were news crews with video cameras in front of the courthouse. She hoped that Hank Snow and his lawyers had come to terms with the government.

"Have the parties had a chance to discuss a plea deal?" she asked.

The U.S. attorney stood up to address the court. "It seems, your honor, that we have the wrong man. We would like to dismiss the charges against Hank Snow." The audience reacted with loud whispers.

This was an interesting twist. Judge Lake wondered what the law firm of Kennedy & Raker had on these three world powers?

"I don't understand," Judge Lake said. "How could the U.S. government have the wrong man?"

"A mistake, your honor."

"Mr. Melvin, as chairman of the National Security Council, do you concur?"

"I do."

"And the FBI?"

A young woman who'd been sitting in the back of the room walked up the aisle and handed a folder to Agent Lemming. Judge Lake recognized her. She'd met Liz Raker during the summer at the Knife & Fork restaurant when Judge Stark waved her over to have lunch with them. Judge Stark was as proud of Liz as he would have been of his own granddaughter. Judge Lake wondered what part the young woman played in the scene before her now.

Agent Lemming looked in the folder Liz handed him, then nodded to the U.S. attorney and said, "Yes, your honor, the FBI concurs. Wrong man."

Judge Lake knew that if the U.S. Attorney's office, the National Security Council, the FBI and two foreign governments were content with this result, she could free the defendant with a clean conscience. But, with a nod to her old friend Judge Stark, she couldn't let the government off that easy.

"I'm disappointed in the government," Judge Lake said. "You accused the defendant of a felony, fought against releasing him on bond and let him sit in jail for almost three months. The only thing you can say is, 'wrong man'?"

Judge Lake picked up her gavel and held it in her hand. "I will allow the government's motion to dismiss the charges on the condition that it pay defendant restitution of one thousand dollars a day for his time in jail. Any objection?"

The U.S. attorney said, "That's more than 80 thousand dollars. I don't have the authority to—"

Melvin interrupted. "That's fine, your honor. The government will pay it."

Judge Lake was ready to rule when she noticed Hank Snow was standing. "Mr. Snow, do you have something you want to say?" Judge Lake asked.

"Yes. If it's not too much trouble, your honor, I'd like to donate the restitution money to the local Salvation Army. The government can drop the check into one of those red Christmas kettles tonight. After all, it's Christmas Eve."

"A very Nice gesture," Judge Lake said. She winked at Snow before slamming her gavel to the bench. "Case dismissed," she said. "The defendant is free to go and make this world a better place. Merry Christmas, everyone!"

Epilogue

December 24ᵗʰ - One Year Later

Liz was impressed with the large turnout at the courthouse for the unveiling of Judge Stark's portrait. Most of the lawyers in town had come to pay their respects. Liz overheard Raker joke that this was the one time they weren't scared to appear in front of the judge.

Liz and Sarah arrived early with Raker. Rule 1 of Judge Stark's Rules of Court: Show up on time.

Judge Johnson was now senior administrative judge and required to be present, but he didn't look comfortable. Liz thought his handshake felt like a limp fish. As if he had nothing to fight for, or against, now that Judge Stark was gone.

After Liz helped to save Christmas the year before, she had gone back to school in a doctoral program and she and her dad had planned this ceremony for Christmas break. She stood off to the side with some friends who'd made an even longer trip. She stood with Hank Snow and Tarina Winter, recently elected chairman and vice chairman of the Elf High Council at Santa's Greenland village, known as North Pole East. Henry Edmonds, now in charge of all Naughty and Nice list collectors as well as being backup Santa, also stood with her and so did Twirly Masters, now director of Santa's worldwide distribution system and the official spokesperson regarding the recent merger of Tip Top Toy Company and North Pole Enterprises.

The elves who never gave up were with her, too: Snowflake, Holly and Mistletoe. Snowflake still had her official role as head of The Archives—preserving the names and data of True Believers around the world—and the responsibility for managing SantaLeaks for Hank Snow, in case the service was ever needed. Mistletoe had been promoted to the director of Reindeer Care, including the responsibility for organizing the annual reindeer games.

Holly now had a new role as chairman of the National Elf Relations Board and custodian of the Reindeer Hoverboards, lest they ever be needed again.

Before the ceremony started, Liz collected her dad, Sarah and Austin Land—members of the BTB—to join her and her magical friends for a short presentation. When everyone was together, she handed a small rectangular box—held tight by red and green ribbon—to Hank Snow. It had a card inside, signed by everyone in the Band of True Believers, and a plaque that read, "Hank Snow, Honorary Member of the Band of True Believers. In Gratitude for Your Lifelong Service to All Who Believe in the Magic of Christmas."

"Welcome to the BTB," Liz said. "We wouldn't have a purpose without you."

She saw his lips tremble and gave him a big hug, which he returned. He proudly showed his plaque to his sister and fellow Christmas workers.

When the clock struck 10, Ralph the bailiff did what Twirly Masters would call a splendid rendition of the oyez speech, opening court without once looking at his notes. It was probably a first in his career. He and the other bailiffs were well-dressed, as if their clothes had just come from the cleaners.

No doughnut stains on their ties. No coffee spills on their pants.

A group of judges in robes walked down the aisle and took reserved seats in the front rows. They included all the local magistrates, a number of state court judges and federal Judge J. P. Lake.

Raker stepped forward and addressed the crowd. "Good morning. Welcome to this ceremony to honor Judge Augustus Langhorne Stark."

Liz looked at an empty space above the judge's bench where a picture once had hung. Raker had told her the story about the portrait that was there the previous December. After a gavel and a hoverboard had gone through it, it couldn't be repaired. Unfortunate, but it left the perfect spot for Judge Stark's portrait.

Tarina whispered to Liz and Snow, "You think Judge Johnson will enjoy having Judge Stark look over his shoulder every day?" They laughed.

"Even in death," Snow said, "Judge Stark will haunt that man."

Raker looked at his notes. "Those of you who appeared in front of Judge Stark over the years— and that's most of you in this room—know that he had 10 rules of court. I always thought he created the rules to help young lawyers navigate the trial process without making fools of themselves. But the more I've thought about his rules, the more I believe he was trying to do more. When he talked about such things as preparation, courtesy, speaking clearly, being a good listener and picking your battles, he was telling us he wanted us to be good lawyers—good citizens—not just juris doctor cage fighters. He wanted us to be Nice."

Raker turned the page on his notes. "His last rule was the one that summed up the rest: Maintain Your Credibility. When I was with him at the end—" Raker's voice broke as he choked back emotion. Gathering himself, he smiled. "Lord knows, he could be stubborn. He pulled that credibility rule on me when he was dying to make me tell him the truth about his condition." Raker paused. "Fact is, credibility and Judge Stark went hand in hand. You knew what you were getting with Judge Stark. An honest man."

Raker held up the morning newspaper. "If you haven't seen this yet, you should read Austin Land's thoughtful article about Judge Stark's positive impact on the justice system. It's an excellent tribute to his career." Raker folded the newspaper and placed it on the lectern. "Besides being a great judge," Raker said, "Judge Stark had a fulfilling life.

You wouldn't know it by his gruff demeanor, but he was a man who loved. He loved his wife. His church. His hobbies. And he loved his beliefs."

Raker smiled at Liz and the rest of the Band of True Believers. "As some of you know, Judge Stark came to one of his beliefs late in life, but from then on, he always believed. In so doing, he found a way to live life to the fullest. To the very end." Raker paused one last time. "It's something we should all do."

Raker motioned to Liz to join him. "I've asked my daughter, Liz, to unveil the portrait. She was very close to Judge Stark."

Liz stepped up to the easel holding the portrait and pulled back the cover. The image of the once stern jurist stared back at the audience but he had a slight, almost imperceptible, smile on his face, as if he knew something they didn't. The audience stood and clapped.

Raker whispered to Liz, "Kind of looks like a True Believer."

"I agree," Liz said. "It's perfect."

She walked back to stand beside Snow. "You hired the recruiter who sent me to Greenland, didn't you?" Snow didn't answer. He just smiled as he watched Ralph the bailiff hang Judge Stark's portrait.

"It's time," Snow said, "that I told you where I hid the second copy of that government document, our leverage to protect Christmas in perpetuity." He nodded toward the portrait that now dominated the courtroom from its place of honor.

Liz looked up at Judge Stark's image and said, "You're kidding." She laughed at the thought of the document inside the back of Judge Stark's portrait. "You couldn't have picked a better place."

"I agree," Tarina said. She stepped forward and patted her little brother on the back.

Sarah moved to the front of the room to fulfill Liz's request. Until this morning, no one except Liz knew the name of Judge Stark's favorite hymn. It was one of the secrets he had shared with her that earlier today she confided in Sarah.

As Sarah started to sing the hymn, the courtroom became reverent. Her voice filled the room and appeared to reach beyond to the heavens, sending goosebumps down Liz's neck and arms. The audience sang the chorus. Judges, bailiffs, lawyers. Friends, adversaries, enemies. Even Judge Cleve R. Johnson.

When the song ended, Liz was crying. Hank Snow reached over and held her hand. There wasn't a dry eye in the courtroom. One by one, everyone in the room came to hug her, to say something Nice about Judge Stark.

At last it was over and only Liz, her dad and Sarah remained. They joined arms, with Liz in the middle, and exited the courtroom together. As they walked away, Liz heard Ralph the bailiff say, "That was the best rendition of 'I'll Fly Away' I ever heard, and the only time I heard it sung in the county courthouse."

Liz smiled to herself as she started to hum Judge Stark's favorite Christmas song. After all, it was Christmas Eve, and Santa Claus was coming to town.

Honorable Judge
Augustus Langhorne Stark

The End

A Note to You, the Reader, from Landis Wade

Thank you for reading *The Christmas Redemption* – I hope the story put you in the Christmas spirit. If you liked this book, please add a review on Amazon or Goodreads. And please tell your friends. Your kind words of support will help other readers find the book.

If you haven't read the first two books in *The Christmas Courtroom Adventure* series, I invite you to do so. Both are free-standing legal mysteries. In *The Christmas Heist,* Thad Raker defends Henry Edmonds in a criminal case to be decided by Judge Augustus Langhorne Stark, at a time when Judge Stark has no patience for a man who claims to work for Santa Claus. In *The Legally Binding Christmas,* Raker represents Twirly Masters in a civil case to be decided by a jury, concerning an old house with a Christmas secret. The books have Christmas courtroom drama mixed with humor, quirky dialogue, odd plot twists and (spoiler alert) happy endings.

This three-book series got started in 2014 on Thanksgiving weekend when my wife Janet was watching the movie, *Miracle on 34ᵗʰ Street*. When I walked into the den, the courtroom scene was underway, the one in which the lawyer is able to convince the judge that his client is the one and only Santa Claus. After laughing once again, I said to myself, "I wonder if I can write a modern-day Christmas story set entirely in the courtroom." I went to my study, sat down at the computer and started writing *The Christmas Heist*. I'm especially thankful for that moment in time and the fact that I finished that story. It introduced me to a new group of friends: readers, writers, book people and characters I never would have met otherwise.

So how does an author say good-bye to a series? What's the right number of books? I thought about it and decided, it had to be three. Besides saving Christmas three times, I needed to deal with Hank Snow and I knew that if I wrote a fourth in the series, I would get more attached to my characters and not know when to stop. Plus, lots of fun things come in threes: Three Little Pigs; Three Stooges; Three Ring Circus; Three Musketeers; Three Strikes You're Out; the Truth, the Whole Truth and Nothing but the Truth; and, being ever so optimistic about breaking even with a third book, Third Time's a Charm.

As I think about what to write next, I would love to hear from you. Here are several ways we can stay in touch:

Sign up at my website: www.landiswade.com

On Facebook: www.facebook.com/thechristmasheist

Email me: landiswrites@gmail.com

Check me out on Amazon, Goodreads, Twitter, YouTube and Pinterest

In the meantime, may the magic of the Christmas season lift you up each and every day. Always Believe!

Acknowledgements

I'm grateful to the *The Christmas Courtroom Adventure* team for their hard work on this book. This year, and for the past three years, they've helped my characters perform the difficult task of saving Christmas: Lystra Books & Literary Services, publisher; Susanne Discenza Frueh (Norman, Oklahoma), illustrator; Nora Gaskin Esthimer (Chapel Hill, North Carolina), editor; Karen Van Neste Owen (Richmond, Virginia), copy editor; and Beth Tashery Shannon the Frogtown Bookmaker (Georgetown, Kentucky), book designer.

I'm also grateful for early feedback provided by the members of the Charlotte Writers' Club's short story critique group, with extra special thanks to two members of the group, Brooke Reynolds and Nick White, who read the entire manuscript when it was 10,000 words longer than it should have been.

Thanks, also, to the talented authors who gave generously of their time to read the manuscript and write the reviews in the front of this book, and also, to those of you who read advance copies and wrote reviews in the cyber-world.

Thanks to Sally Brewster and the staff at Park Road Books and Adah Fitzgerald and the staff at Main Street Books for your support and advice with the entire series.

Thanks to my daughter, Jordan, who read and gave feedback on this book before it went to the design phase and to my son, Hamlin, whose travels to such ice-covered places as the Norwegian archipelago of Svalbard were an inspiration for staging parts of this story in remote northern locations. Thanks also to my wife, Janet, who used her skills as a long-time fifth grade teacher to suggest improvements to the book, while also noticing interesting mistakes, like how I "refilled" tea glasses with water and put Tarina Winter in a courtroom scene at the same time she was in jail with Hank Snow.

Finally, thanks to all my family, friends and colleagues for your love and support with the series and to you, the reader, for spending some of your valuable time with me on my whimsical courtroom journey to save Christmas.

Landis Wade is a civil trial lawyer, arbitrator, mediator and author in Charlotte, N.C. He is a 1979 graduate of Davidson College, where he majored in history and played varsity football, and a 1983 graduate of Wake Forest Law School, where he was a member of the Law Review and the National Moot Court team. Landis is married, has two adult children and two rescue dogs. He enjoys sports, traveling with his family, and spending time at their cabin in Watauga County, N.C., where he likes to fly-fish, hike, bike, read and write.

Visit the webpage: www.landiswade.com

Visit the Facebook page:
www.facebook.com/thechristmasheist.

Contact the author: landiswrites@gmail.com